HOLIDAY AFFAIRS

An Erotica Collection

T0337285

mischief

Mischief
An imprint of HarperCollins*Publishers*
77–85 Fulham Palace Road,
Hammersmith, London W6 8JB

www.mischiefbooks.com

A Paperback Original 2013

First published in Great Britain in ebook format by
HarperCollins*Publishers* 2012

A catalogue record for this book is
available from the British Library

ISBN-13: 9780007553303

Find out more about HarperCollins and the environment at
www.harpercollins.co.uk/green

CONTENTS

Pass Me Around
Giselle Renarde   1

Heat
Charlotte Stein   18

Lust from the Mummy's Tomb
Rose de Fer   32

The Big Gift
Valerie Grey   50

Layover
Jeremy Edwards   67

Caribbean Heat
Kathleen Tudor   84

Polar Bear Passion
Heather Towne   102

Welcome to Spain
Chrissie Bentley   120

Cruise Control
Elizabeth Coldwell   136

Christmas in the Caribbean
Jacqueline Seewald   152

Pass Me Around
Giselle Renarde

I'd never done anything so dangerous.

I blame the four-hour car trip with my cousin and her giggling gaggle of girlfriends. They annoyed the hell out of me, playing music by some stupid pop music idol I'd never heard of – same song on repeat, played seventeen times over. Yes, I was counting. Anything was better than listening to their inane conversations about makeup and fad diets and celebrity pets.

By the time we got to our campsite, I was so full of irritation I took off for a jog while the other girls pitched our tent. They weren't too happy with me but, after so long in the car, my muscles were desperate for motion. That, and the girls' squeaky baby-doll voices were driving me nuts.

We were lucky to get a site in what the park called 'The Pines', the section with the most secluded camping spots. In other areas of the campground, you could see your neighbours the minute you stepped out of your tent. My family used to come here on vacation when I was a kid, so I knew it well. In 'The Pines', you had to go a fair stretch to pitch your tent or park your trailer. It was nice to have all that privacy.

On my reluctant way back to my cousin and the girls, I heard voices from the campsite next to ours. Guys' voices. Lots of them. They were laughing, joking around, having a good time. As soon as I heard the jocular tone of those men's voices, a tingle ran through me. More than a tingle, actually – my entire belly lit up! I don't know if I'd been spending too much time around other women or if it had just been way too long since I'd gone home with a guy, but I burned for what they had. I wanted it.

I should have checked in with my cousin and her little friends. They'd surely be wondering where I'd gone, right? Well, maybe not. My cousin and I had been penpal BFFs since we were little, but her gal pals didn't seem to like me very much. When you're from The Big Smoke, the rest of the country is predisposed to hating you. It's almost like they're jealous that you live in an economic and cultural centre, while they spend their date nights making out in their boyfriends' trucks. Whatever the reason, I'd learned that if you lived in a big city, you would naturally become the target of widespread malice.

Maybe that's why I lied to those guys about where I was from, once I'd worked up the courage to approach their campsite. I'm not a liar by nature, but when I walked up that long stretch of pine needles and caught sight of those six guys drinking Moosehead around the fire, I knew I had to have them.

All of them.

'Hey,' was all I could think to say. Stupid, but I needed to show them I wasn't lost. I meant to be there. I knew what I was getting myself into, and I wasn't as innocent as I appeared.

The guys all looked up at me from their folding chairs. Six men around one fire pit. Twelve eyes. All on me. I felt ravaged already.

The day had been hot, and I'd worn cut-offs and a halter top short enough to show off my belly ring. I could tell by the guys' dark expressions that the outfit was a good choice. They just stared at me, stammering, 'Hey' while their jaws swept the fireside.

'Can I bum a beer?' I asked, grabbing a bottle from their cooler and popping the top off against the picnic table.

I watched them watching me as I took a long pull on the beer, letting a few drops slide out the side of my mouth, drizzle down my chin and drip into my cleavage. The cold liquid felt good against my overheated chest, and I could tell without looking that my braless tits were getting hard, my pink little nipples standing erect underneath my halter top. I could pass for a country girl.

One of the guys, tan and fit with a Celtic tattoo around his bicep, was smart enough to ask, 'How old are you?'

The question made me laugh, and I let a little cascade of beer spill out of the bottle and on to my breasts, just to draw their gazes away from my face. 'Twenty-three?'

That was such a lie. I was actually twenty-seven, but I got the feeling some of these guys might be younger than me, and the older-woman dynamic wasn't one I wished to encourage. I wanted them thinking I was cute and naïve, just like all my cousin's stupid friends. Maybe if I could convince them I was nice and young, they'd think this whole six-on-one situation would be something new for me.

As if!

The guys weren't saying anything, so it was up to me to lure them in. No problem. Male energy was a sex toy, something I could pick up and roll between my fingers, something dynamic and changeable, just like a cock.

Weaving between their folding chairs, I drank my beer, sensing their eyes like sunshine all over my bare legs. I had a feeling these guys weren't from the city, so I lied and said I lived in Huntsville, crossing my fingers that they'd have no comments or follow-up questions. Luckily, they didn't. Or maybe they were so quiet because, as I told my lie, I bent at the hips, bent all the way down to pick a sheet of birch bark off the ground. The guys behind me would have had a nice view of the swell of my ass in those itty-bitty shorts. And the guys in front of me? They held their collective breath, waiting to see if my braless breasts might slip out of my halter top.

The sexual tension was palpable, like a thick film on the air. I could taste it, and it danced on my tongue, sweet as chocolate. More, I wanted more, more, more!

I tossed the birch bark on the fire and it went up in a tall blaze. What an amazing spectacle. I wanted to be like that, an instant flame. Touch me and I'm on fire.

The guy with the Celtic tattoo asked me what my name was, and I said, 'Candy.'

Candy.

I don't know why I picked that one, except that it suited the way I felt in the moment. In all probability, they suspected it was a fake, or at best a nickname, but by then my head was spinning. Maybe I'd stood up too fast after bending down, or maybe it was the beer, but I couldn't think straight. All I knew was that if I didn't get fucked by each and every one of these guys, I'd go crazy.

Hey, who knows? Maybe I'd already gone.

Night descended quickly, and I wondered if my cousin was worried now the light was growing dim. Probably not. Our site wasn't far away, and they could probably hear me through the trees. Maybe they were listening while I told this group of hot young studs that I was a lingerie model.

I'd never told so many lies back to back, and it scared me how easily they came. Crazy as it seemed, I'd have done anything to get those boys inside of me. Just the sight of their bodies in shades of gold and brown had my pussy pulsing against the seam of my cut-offs. Every time I shifted even a little bit, my shorts rode up my crotch, stroking my clit. The wetness defied belief.

And these boys had some of the most incredible bodies I'd ever seen. Their naked chests gleamed with sweat in the early evening heat, and their muscular arms twitched as they clung to their beers. I imagined their hands wrapped not around bottles but around the undoubtedly hard cocks beneath their swimsuits. The very image of those boys pumping their massive erections made my knees buckle.

I didn't ask them any questions about themselves, like what their names were or where they were from. To be honest, I didn't care. I just hoped one of them might make a move, but I guess I knew I'd have to do all the work. They were just waiting for it.

When I'd finished my first beer, I took another one and said, 'Guys, I'm so horny. It really sucks.' Without another word, I drank up.

The guys looked at me like I was crazy, or like I was trying to get them locked up – which I probably should have expected.

'Is this a trick?' the darkest of the six guys asked.

I shook my head, trying to look innocent – but not *too* innocent. 'Nah, no tricks. I just need a good fuck. You guys know where I can find one?'

Disbelief.

A few of them laughed in a way that seemed to mean, 'Is this chick for real?' I'm sure they had no idea, but the music of their scepticism only egged me on.

The sun was setting fast, but the guys' faces were clearly visible by the light of the campfire, their hard chests and bare legs painted orange by the flickering flames. Suddenly one of them laughed and then pressed his hand against his lips to stifle the sound. The rest of them were quiet as church mice.

What, did I have to beg for it?

'Come on, you guys.' I put on a pout. 'I really, really want it. Give a dog a bone?'

The same guy who'd laughed before laughed again, and then rose on unsteady feet. 'Hey, I'm game,' he said. 'I'll give you what I got.'

He wasn't the hottest of the bunch – paler skin than the rest, and frizzy orange hair – but the firelight tempted me. Stepping over another guy's feet, I went to the frizzy boy, spurred on by the heat of the fire and the humid warmth hanging on the air.

Where to begin?

The boy who'd called me over wore a snarky sort of grin, which made me want to punch him more than kiss him, so I decided to ignore his face. Instead, I zeroed in on his flat white chest and licked a nipple. It tasted salty, which was no surprise, but I was amazed at how erect his little pink bud grew as I teased it. In no time, his nipple was hard as a pencil eraser, jutting out far enough that I could actually suck it! Hopefully I was making the other guys jealous, but I couldn't tell if my wicked ways were working through their hush.

So I looked at the next guy in the circle. His brown skin glowed with the heat of the flames, and he looked like he was hypnotised. Winking, I said to him, 'I really want to touch your friend's cock. Do you think he'll let me?'

'Shit yeah, I'll let you!' Just like that the frizzy-haired dude dropped his shorts and his erection sprang up to greet me. 'You can do whatever you want to it!'

Until that moment, I hadn't felt bashful in the least. I was play-acting after all, taking on the role of the nympho, the slut, the seductress. It wasn't until Frizzy dropped his swim trunks that the reality hit me: I'd given myself over to six strangers and there was no turning back. Either I grabbed that dick or I ran away with my tail between my legs.

My heart seized in my chest as I stared at Frizzy's erection, wondering if his pubes were really that red or if it was just the fire that made them look that way. Not that it mattered. I was just buying time, I realised, nego-tiating with myself. If I didn't act soon, the guys would see right through me. They'd know I wasn't Candy the lingerie model from Huntsville, and I was desperate to keep up the act. *Desperate.*

Without another moment's hesitation, I took Frizzy's nice-sized cock in hand and pumped that solid slab of meat. He groaned as I jerked him off, cupping his big fuzzy balls and squeezing gently. His arousal sparked my aggression, and suddenly I knew I could go ahead with this without fear. I could give myself over to my lust and theirs.

'Any of you guys got condoms with you?' I asked so loudly half the campground probably heard.

One guy took off to a tent, nearly tripping over his feet as he watched me stroke his buddy's cock. He came back with a big box of condoms, which sort of made me wonder what these dudes had planned to do if I hadn't randomly wandered onto their site.

'Pass 'em around,' I said, eyeing the Trojans. 'And then when you're done, you can pass me around.'

The guys were auspiciously silent as they suited up, kicked their swim trunks away from the flames and rearranged the camp chairs. Even the eager frizzy-haired boy whose cock I was stroking hadn't ventured to touch me. Not once. In truth, their hesitancy put me at ease.

I looked at these gorgeous golden, bronze and brown young men standing naked in a circle, and my heartbeat fell into my pussy. I was so damn hot for them I tore out of my halter top and threw down my cut-offs and panties in one swift motion. The night was warm, and the fire baked my skin, but that was nothing compared to the blazing heat of my cunt. I wanted them in there, all of them – now!

'Hey, what's the hold-up?' I met their lustful yet apprehensive gazes all around the circle. 'What, you want me to do everything? You boys are hard and ready, so let's go!'

I pressed Frizzy into a chair turned away from the fire, got down on my knees and slipped his dick right down my throat. He obviously wasn't expecting me to swallow him whole, but all the other guys had already put on condoms and I never did like the flavour of latex. Summer sweat tinged with the hot aroma of man was more to my taste. I sucked that dick while he sat motionless, like what I was doing scared the life out of him. Maybe he'd never had his dick sucked before. Maybe Frizzy was a virgin! Imagine that …

I glanced quickly around the circle, and it sort of pissed me off that everyone was standing still. Didn't they want me? Wasn't I hot?

'Would somebody please fuck me, already? I'm tired of waiting.' With that, I turned my attention back to devouring the cock in front of me. I didn't want to see who took his turn first. I wanted to get fucked completely anonymously.

The men closed in after my outburst, and every time

I glanced up from Frizzy's firm cock I saw their massive erections moving closer, bouncing against thick pillows of hairy balls as they approached. Somebody grabbed my hips then, yanking me from the dusty ground until I was standing on both feet. Guess these boys didn't want to get their knees dirty! The motion threw me harder against Frizzy's dick, and I swallowed it deeper than I would have thought possible. I had to grab his wiry thighs for support, afraid I'd tumble forward, knocking us both into the flames.

And then I felt it: some guy's cock inching its way inside of me, pushing its mushroom tip slowly before filling me up with its massive shaft. I didn't look back to see who was fucking me. I didn't care who it was. These guys were just sexual bystanders, convenient cocks, and I was putting them to good use. I closed my eyes and concentrated on the one that was throbbing against my tongue, getting bigger by the second.

Just as soon as I started bucking back against whoever was filling my cunt, Mister Frizzy's little thighs started to quake. 'Oh, fuck!' he kept saying, grasping the folding chair's plastic arms so hard I was sure he'd break them off. 'Oh fuck, not yet!'

I didn't want him to come yet either, but if he insisted, I really didn't want him to come down my throat. I pulled his big dick from my mouth and aimed his cockhead at my tits. Naked, they beckoned and waved with the motion of someone-or-other fucking me from behind. I pumped Frizzy's dick as hard and fast as my hand would let me, hoping he'd spill his seed against my pink little nipples. He came in wild white streaks, coating my neck and one of my breasts with jizz, and that was good enough for me. I didn't even wipe it off.

As soon as he was spent, I called out, 'I need another dick!'

Somebody pushed the chair with Frizzy still in it out of the way and caught me as I plummeted towards the ground. This guy, one of the golden boys, held me up by my tits, one hand sliding where my breast was covered in jizz. I tore off his condom and grabbed hold of his hard ass as he slid his long cock down my throat. If I didn't have such great control over my gag reflex, his length would have made me spew. I preferred a thick dick to a long one, but I couldn't complain with my mouth full.

The two guys fucking me, one in my pussy and the other in my mouth, took over the motion and I just let them do as they pleased. I kept getting this weird image of my body as one of those long lumber saws and the two guys as lumberjacks at either end of me. This is what I'd wanted from the very beginning: for them to take control and use me like a toy. Took long enough to get them there!

The huge cock filling my pussy reamed me at double speed. The guy groaned, 'Fuck yeah, I'm coming! I'm coming!'

'Come!' I encouraged him, speaking around the cock in my mouth. I forced my ass back into the saddle of his hips.

Digging his fingers into my ass cheeks, that guy rammed me hard. When he came, I nearly pushed Golden Boy into the woods.

Whoever had just creamed his condom obviously knew the drill, because he cleared the path for the next guy without waiting for me to say anything. Golden Boy was obviously brought near to the edge hearing his friend's cries of 'Fuck yeah!' and 'I'm coming!' because his breathing grew strained and his motion ceased altogether. I grabbed his shaft with one hand and sucked hard on his deep red cockhead, daring him to come.

'On your tits!' Golden Boy begged.

Doubling over, he pressed my boobs together so hard it hurt, but who was I to shy away from a little pain? I smooshed my face against his hot, hard pelvis so he could get close enough to shove his dick into the softness of my cleavage. Once he'd lodged his erection between my tits, I licked his belly and he came straightaway. His cream was still dripping down my front when another guy stepped forward to take his place.

And a second guy beside him. They were going to double-team my face, and all I could do was smile.

Someone had set a blanket on the ground, and every man around lowered me onto it until I was perched there on my hands and knees. I'd lost count by then. How many of these guys had fucked me? How many of them had come? Three of the six? Now there was one guy in my pussy, his dick obviously smaller than the last guy's because the sensation barely registered, and two more shoving their cocks in my face.

If this wasn't heaven, I didn't know what heaven was!

The guys kneeling in front of me tore out of their condoms and aimed their cocks so close together their heads actually touched. The sight made my whole body moan. My pussy clenched tight, milking the guy who was frantically pumping inside of it. He grabbed my hips and fucked me harder.

'You guys!' I gasped before trying to fit my lips around two cockheads at once. 'God, this is so fucking hot, you guys.'

'Yeah,' they all agreed, and I felt someone's beer spill across my back while somebody else smacked my ass.

Sucking two dicks at once was no easy task. I was afraid my teeth might sink into their erections deep enough to cause them pain, but I was really careful and the guys made no complaints. I licked the place where their two cocks met in my mouth, all the while pumping their shafts with frenzied vigour, trying to stroke them both with just one hand.

Their cocks were just too much for me. I had to suck them in alternation, feeling all those men's eyes on my mouth as I wrapped my lips around one cockhead and then the other. The insistent thrusting from behind forced me forward, and I swallowed so much cock that I gagged a bit. I had to steel myself against the solid bangs.

Just when I thought the four of us had developed a rhythm, the guy in my pussy pulled out. Right away, I felt his cockhead pressing against my asshole and I screamed around the hard dick in my mouth.

He didn't ask if he should stop, which surprised me, and although I knew I'd pay with searing pain, getting fucked up the ass without proper lubrication, I wanted the sheer exhilaration more than I could bear. Still, I didn't let myself look back. I knew how much this was going to hurt.

To my surprise, I felt a slick, familiar liquid drizzling down my ass crack. It was lube! Someone was dousing me in lube, preparing for a smooth entry. Once I was good and slick, the guy behind me, whoever he was, pressed his cockhead into my ass. He should have gone slower. He should have taken his time. It burned like hell, but I didn't give a fuck. I bucked back against him, feeling the blaze spread until my thighs shook. He was hissing and then howling, digging his fingers into the flesh of my ass cheeks.

The guy behind me worked his dick into my asshole, thrusting relentlessly, and in time the ache shifted into pressure. I tried not to think about it. I refocused on the two dicks right in front of me, sucking one, then the other. The harder I worked at those boys, the more the pressure in my ass began to feel a lot like pleasure. Yes, it was … it was good! I pushed back against the guy behind me, giving him my ass like a gift, wanting to feel this sensation all week.

Sitting up as straight as I could, I aimed the two cocks in front of me at my tits. The pose was just too awkward with a dick up my ass, so I let the guys take over, aiming their cocks wherever they liked. They took turns feeding their erections to me and jerking off against my cheeks. I sucked so hard I thought I'd take the skin off, but they both seemed to like it. There was such a frenzy of lust that I'm not even sure who came first, but by the time it was all over there was come in my hair and dripping down both my shoulders. The guy in my ass took a while to pull, but there were no more hard cocks to satisfy me, so I didn't mind.

When the strangers were spent and I was covered in come, they arranged their seats around the fire and tossed a few more logs on top of it to get the flames roaring again. Everyone was quiet, but the crackling flames sounded like laughter to my ears and I wondered if it was mocking me. But why would it? I knew what I wanted and I got it.

I picked up my clothes and dressed, feeling somewhat sheepish. They guys were still naked, and they all looked amazing. For a while I sat on my blanket, staring into the flames and gazing from face to face, but I was no longer the centre of attention so I decided it was time to go.

When I said my goodbyes, the guys stammered, 'Thanks,' and 'See you later, Candy.'

It took a moment before I remembered that was me.

Heat
Charlotte Stein

I come up from below expecting to be alone, but I'm not.
Hunter is inexplicably there, sprawled on a sun lounger
with his big feet trailing off the end, that stupid handsome hair of his gleaming in the glare.

And all I can think is: I wish his name wasn't Hunter.
I've never in my life known anyone called anything like
that, and I don't feel like starting now. It's just so … beef-
cake. It's so … Abercrombie and Fitch, even though I'm
British and barely know what Abercrombie and Fitch is.

I don't want to know. I just want to sit on the sun
lounger he's currently occupying and read my book, like
a semi-normal person. I'm the sort who goes on sun-
blistering holidays somewhere exotic, and then sits alone
beneath a giant umbrella to shelter themselves from the
heat – and I won't apologise for that.

But Hunter makes me apologise. He looks up the

18

moment I'm on deck, and smiles his winning smile, and says something I don't want to hear, like 'I was wondering when you'd join me.' As though there's a possibility that *we* could actually join. The universe is making new glue as we speak, for bookworms who refuse to wear bathing suits and giant jockish men called *Hunter*.

He's out of his mind – perhaps literally. Lily says he's secretly weird, that he has trouble relating to people, that his parents died years ago and ever since he's been some kind of hermit ... but I don't buy it. People like him aren't hermits.

They're on the covers of catalogues, staring off at imaginary horizons. He doesn't need this holiday. He doesn't need to socialise. He needs to spend five thousand dollars on deck shoes, before insulting some waiter we don't have.

Hell, maybe I'm the waiter, in this scenario. I certainly feel like one as I edge around his most glorious self, in an attempt to reach the sun lounger on the other side of the deck.

But then I see it, and suddenly I'm not a waiter at all. I'm trapped into being his holiday companion, by the presence of the seat he's moved next to himself. He's actually dragged it all the way across this bright-white deck to make a neat little pair, side by side.

As though that's perfectly reasonable.

He even makes it sound reasonable.

'Come and sit down,' he says, which of course gives

me no choice. If I say no, I'll look anti-social and awful. And if I say yes … if I say yes …

I'll have to sit next to him, right next to him, with the heat of the sun blasting me on one side and the heat from him blasting me on the other. In fact, I can practically feel it before I've even taken the lounger next to him. He's so bright, so big, so winning – he makes the sun look like a speck on the face of a giant.

He's the giant in question.

He's so big that I feel crowded the second I arrange myself on the lounger, even though he's set them a decent way apart. I can get my whole hand between them without any trouble at all, but that's not the point when your companion is eight foot eleven. His arms span that tiny gap with very little effort, and any time he shifts a tad I can just feel him.

I can feel the heat coming off him, in waves. I can smell his suntan lotion, light and summery, and the febrile scent of his skin beneath. Sunshine skin, my mother would have called it – and it is. You can tell the kind of tan he has just from drinking in that scent: a golden honey hovering over the blush underneath.

But of course I have to confirm how it looks, anyway. I pretend I'm engrossed in my book, when really I can't stop flicking my gaze to his immense hands – pale on the inside, caramel on the out. He's fiddling with the tie on his shorts, which only makes the show more compelling.

Those long fingers, those heavy knuckles … and then further down the endless stretch of his solid legs. I confess, I follow them all the way to his feet, which aren't clad in the five-thousand-dollar deck shoes. They're bare, instead, completely bare, and somehow that's much worse.

His feet are even more gigantic than his hands, and knuckly like them, too. They're a real man's feet – different to Patrick's, all neat and clean. They make me think that he's not an airbrushed-catalogue-model Hunter, at all, but a real one instead.

He goes into the forest, at night, and runs down a hapless deer. And then when the moon is at its fullest, he tears the thing apart, with his teeth. He tears me apart, with his teeth. He makes me want to look at his face, but I can't, I can't.

Why isn't he saying anything now?

He wanted me to sit, didn't he? He wanted me to join him, in that tiring way most middle-class people with yachts seem to demand. Patrick needs it all the time, and so does Lily, and so does Gregory – though I know there's something different between the time they want from me and the time Hunter does.

I can feel it prickling in the air, now, between the words he thought he should say and the silence he now allows. He doesn't want idle chitchat, I think. He wants to sit here and make me bake in his heat, until I'm so uncomfortable I could die.

And then he abruptly puts a hand on my thigh, and I think I *do* die. I stop breathing, at the very least, because he's not low down, towards my knee. He's really, really high up – almost under my sundress, in fact.

And when I don't move away or slap him or any of the things I should do, he slides that hand higher, casually. Like he's just turning the pages of a book he's not all that interested in. It could even be the book I've just discarded, which is now lying on the floor by my lounger.

Either way – I could almost pretend he isn't doing this at all. I don't look at him. He doesn't speak. There are no questions, no answers. Just his hand working further and further up my thigh, until finally he's clasping me in a very rude place indeed.

I can feel the webbing between his thumb and forefinger, pressing tight against the taut mound of my pussy. And after a second of this, I can make out that finger rubbing in slow circles, right between my legs.

It makes me very, very aware of my greedy little hole. It's like he's feeling for the right spot, or maybe suggesting where it might be, through the material of my panties – and he's right too. That is where my cunt resides, and further up oh further up … yesss. That's where my clit is.

But he doesn't linger there for long, either. He alternates back and forth, stroking over my hole and then back over my clit, as though testing which one I like best. I can't decide, however. The former is so rude, so ... humiliating, somehow, while the latter simply sparks pleasure up the length of my spine.

Both sensations are utterly, deliriously delicious. I want to spread my legs wider just to get more of them, but of course I restrain myself. It's bad enough that I'm letting him rub me like this, without saying a word – as though he's so handsome and magnificent that he just has a right to my helpless body.

Egging him on is completely out of the question. I can't even look at him.

Until I do, and then ... then I wish I hadn't.

He doesn't seem like himself, any more. He's not a composed cut-out from the cover of a magazine. His eyelids are so heavy it's almost a burden on me to carry them, and his soft lips have parted in this really suggestive way. Even if he wasn't currently stroking my swollen pussy, I'd know what's going on here.

It's like he wants me to reach up and slide something into that open mouth of his, and if I was better at this – more sure of myself, sexier, an adventuress – I'd know what that something was. I'd take it out and fuck his face, until he begged me to stop.

The way I beg him to stop, after a moment of this. I have to, after all. If he keeps going I'll come all in an embarrassing rush, just because he's got a finger on some material and is rubbing me through it.

23

Too bad, really, that my protests come out wordlessly, soundlessly. I barely make it to a syllable. I just lie on the sun lounger and let him work my stiff clit to a shuddery, buckled-down sort of orgasm, while a thin breath takes the place of all the things I want to say.

Stop, I think. Don't, I think.

But I can't get either word out. I'm awash in this brutal kind of pleasure, of the sort that doesn't take kindly to being restrained. It spills around the edges of my control and pushes through the boundaries I've long established, and once a bit of it's free it goes on and on and on.

It's like letting a tidal wave flow through an opening the size of a little finger. And once it's done, the dam wall isn't in particularly good shape. It's cracked and battered and crumbling at the seams, in a way that's obvious to even the most casual of observers.

I can see it in his face, as he draws away from me. His lip is faintly curled and there's a crease between his brows, as though to say: *that's all it takes, to ruin someone like you?* And then when he sits back in his lounger and picks up a magazine – as though nothing happened, nothing at all – I hear his final point loud and clear, even though he doesn't say it out loud.

How disappointing.

* * *

24

I know he's up there. I can hear his big feet pounding around on the deck, but I'm not going to go up. Not this time. I don't know why he keeps staying behind while they go off and explore tourist spots, but in all honesty I don't care.

He can stew up there, alone. He can conjure up some other person to torment – some girl who's more his speed. She's the other half of that magazine cover, and when he puts a hand between her legs she doesn't soak through her knickers immediately. She doesn't twist and shiver beneath his barely-there touch, as though she's just grateful for any human contact.

Instead, she eyes him coldly, indifferently, while lying there like a statue. Later on they'll make love on the bed behind me, in an elegant, poised sort of way. She'll point her toes and arrange her hair just so on the pillow, and he'll never look at her with that weird combination of incredulity and disdain.

Or at least, that's what I'm still hoping for when he appears in the doorway.

He's probably got her in tow now. I can practically smell her sunshine scent and hear her glassy voice – to the point where I actually start wondering if I should offer to make her a drink, too. I have all the accoutrements in front of me. The bar between the bed and the kitchenette is well stocked with all kinds of lovely things.

And I know, because I'm currently putting all of them together, for myself. I'm calling the rainbow-coloured concoction before me a 'Burn That Sex Thing From Your Memory' daiquiri.

Even though I don't really know what a daiquiri is. It just sounds good, on the end of my imaginary cocktail. It legitimises fluorescent memory-loss in a glass, topped by a raft of candy-coloured cherries – one of which I devour, casually, as he strolls up behind me.

Yeah, that's right. He *strolls*. He's as casual as I am, apparently, even though I'm nothing of the kind. I'm shivering just as I did before, only without the excuse of an orgasm. And as before, I can't really seem to function beyond this. I can't look at him. I just stare straight ahead at the picture on the far wall, of a fisherman who's unaccountably shouldering a huge shotgun.

Or maybe it's not a fisherman, at all. It's just a guy in a vest that looks like a fisherman's, and really he's out to bag himself a nice girl in a white sundress.

Of the kind Hunter then lifts.

I can feel him doing it, somewhere behind me. And I say somewhere, because it's like the whole thing is not attached to me at all. I'm not wearing this sundress. I'm three hundred feet away from myself, drinking a made-up daiquiri.

While a man exposes my almost bare backside, and strokes his big hands over whatever flesh he finds there.

God only knows what he's going to do next. I can't imagine, because I've got no frame of reference for this.

Usually men say things like 'Would you perhaps want to move over to the bed?' or similar, and even those sorts of fellows are in short supply, for a girl of my type. This kind of thing … this kind of silent thievery, heavy with assumption …

I don't know what to do with this.

So I just stand there and take it instead. I let him rub over my ass until he works up to something bolder – both hands under the elastic of my knickers, fondling and fondling me before finally pulling the whole lot down. And then once I'm completely bare under there, he gets hold of me in a tamer sort of place.

Like the hollows of my hips – which only seems tame until he tugs me back. After that, it doesn't seem tame at all. I'm now somehow bent over the bar with my ass bared, and though I don't remember doing it my legs are apart.

They're really, embarrassingly wide apart. I bet he can see everything in between, when he glances down. I bet he can see how wet I am, how swollen my pussy is – though I've no idea why that's the case. He hasn't touched me anywhere in particular. He hasn't said anything filthy, to fire me up.

He just breathes hard and manoeuvres me into position, while my heart thunders between my legs and perspiration gets me in its cloying grip. I'm so hot, I think, so boiling boiling hot, but there's nothing I can do about that.

It's him who has to put the fire out. He has to do something, even though I'm afraid of what that something might be. If he fucks me, I might die. The dam will definitely crumble and my face will never recover from this kind of burn, and that's how it will be until the end of time.

Only it isn't like that at all. When he puts one heavy hand on my shoulder and one heavier hand on my hip, I don't flinch. I'm crying, but I don't want to tell him to stop. I want him to use me up like this, to be that guy who thinks he can have whatever he wants – because God knows he can.

Go on, I think, go on, and then I feel him sliding something thick and solid into my unbearably tight little cunt and ohhhh I can hardly believe it. I can't believe he's actually going to fuck me; I can't believe his cock feels this impossibly big – or that I'm slick enough to take him.

But most of all I can't believe that he moans, as he takes me.

He gets about halfway in and then he just lets it out, low and guttural, thick with frustration. Like he actually wants this, somehow, like he actually needs it, and if he doesn't get it soon he's going to go insane. He's going to shove into me, hard, and fuck me like a savage.

And I don't know whether I'm unhappy about that or not. It sure doesn't feel like unhappiness. It feels like I want to spread my legs wider and take him deeper, and when he finally eases all the way in and groans hot

28

and heavy against the nape of my neck, I do it anyway.

I arch back against him, and spread myself for him, and let him get a handful of my breasts – first one, then the other. Though even that's not enough. I have to fumble with the front of my sundress until the whole thing is open and he can get his hand inside, and once it is it's like a relief. He can get at all of me, now. He can play with my tight nipples as he eases back and forth in my slick cunt – slow and easy at first, but soon it's fast. Soon it's hard and reckless and I'm clutching at the arm he's got across my belly, as he fucks into me. I'm urging him on, without words.

Dear God, there can't be any words for this. There are just moans and guttural grunts and the occasional gasp, when he hits my G-spot just right or I clench a little too tightly around his thick cock. And they get louder, too, the longer this goes on. By the time he's almost got me off the floor and over the bar – pounding me hard with one hand on my hip and the other on my throat – we're like animals.

I'm so wet it's running down my thighs; so turned on I might actually come just from the feel of him fucking into me. And then he gets a hand between my legs and slithers a finger over my swollen, slippery clit – and that's it. I *do* come. I come shamelessly, unlike the day before. I cry out and let myself shake through it, without an ounce of caring in me.

No – it's only afterwards that I care. That I realise what I've done, what I've let myself become. If I was an easy, quick-to-orgasm little slut yesterday, what must I seem like now? I didn't even care whether he wore a condom or not. He could be creaming into my filthy little whore's pussy as I realise all of this – and the thought isn't half as awful as it should be.

In fact, it excites me. I hear him coming, I feel him coming – all jerky and as uncontrolled as I was, a moment before – and I thrill with the idea of him filling me up.

And then it's over, and we're back in the land of condom-wearing and shame-experiencing. I mean, of course he wore a rubber. He wouldn't fuck a thing like me without one and even if he did, there's still that expression on his face that I'm just waiting for. I'll turn around and it'll be there, that mix of disdain and incredulity.

Only when I actually do, his face is not as I remember it. The crease is between his brows, true enough – and that perfect upper lip is curled. But I can't quite make the expression fit into the box marked Magazine Model. It doesn't go with this season's version of Ripe Contempt.

Instead, I see it anew. I feel it anew, as hot as the sun on my skin, as bright as its light in the sky.

He's not disgusted that I would do something like this. He's amazed that I would let him. That's what this is: amazement. I just misread it, because of all the years I've spent studying the covers, instead of the contents.

I don't think he saw daylight for the better part of a year, Lily says, in my head. And then I speak, to make up for all the things I didn't say before. For all the things he obviously can't.

'More,' I tell him. 'Make me feel it. Make me burn.'

Lust from the Mummy's Tomb
Rose de Fer

'So whose tomb are we robbing?'

Sir André Walden frowned. 'We're not robbing anyone's tomb,' he said, turning around from the front seat to fix his niece with a stern schoolmasterly look. 'And I trust you and Peter won't make me regret my decision to allow you in.'

Val matched his frown and nodded with exaggerated seriousness. 'We understand, sir,' she said.

Beside her Peter stifled a laugh and cupped his wife's shapely bottom, making her squirm.

The jeep crested a little rise and sand swirled around them in the warm umber glow of the desert sunset. The Sphinx and the Pyramids were far behind them now and if they were travelling along any kind of road it wasn't at all obvious.

André said something to his assistant, Hossam, in

Arabic and pointed off across the horizon. Hossam glanced back at his passengers and shook his head, shifting gears roughly and making the jeep lurch. A heated conversation ensued which neither Peter nor Val could understand. The Egyptian seemed unhappy with the destination and from André's patronising tone Val guessed that her uncle was telling him off over some silly local superstition.

Eventually Hossam gave in to André and waved a dismissive hand. Peter and Val exchanged a look and shrugged.

'Sorry about that,' André said, turning back to them. 'My assistant objects to "outsiders" being allowed into the tomb before it's been fully explored. He's afraid you won't show the proper respect.' He made it clear by his tone that he shared Hossam's concern.

Peter rolled his eyes. 'Honestly, what is the big deal? We're not bloody grave robbers. We're not going to dig up some mummy and cart it back to London to display in our front room. We just want to take some pictures in the tomb.'

'Yeah, and anyway,' Val said sweetly, 'it'll be great publicity for you. Maybe some rich Egyptophile will give you more money to preserve the tomb. Or whatever.'

André arched an eyebrow at her. 'Or whatever,' he echoed. 'Yes, more publicity is just what Egypt needs. After all, it's not as if thousands of tourists descend on the desert every year, tearing up the landscape and defacing the sites in the hope of stumbling across some priceless find that will make them rich.'

'Come on, we'll be good, we promise. Won't we, Peter?'

'Of course we will. And we promise not to dig anything up. We didn't even bring a shovel.'

'There wasn't any space left in the first-aid kit,' Val added with a wink to her husband.

André eyed them as though certain they were making a joke at his expense. Then his features softened and he shook his head with an indulgent smile.

Pressing the advantage, Peter said, 'So tell us whose tomb it is, then.'

André relented. 'Very well. Her name was Akhenekhbet.'

'*Gezundheit*,' Peter said with a laugh.

'Who?' Val asked.

André gave them both a withering look. 'Akhenekhbet,' he repeated, pronouncing it slowly for them. 'She was a priestess of the vulture goddess Nekhbet.'

'Eww,' Val said, wrinkling her nose.

'You may think "eww", young lady,' André said, 'but the vulture was sacred to the ancient Egyptians, along with plenty of other creatures you'd probably have the same reaction to, like scarab beetles and scorpions.'

'Sorry,' she said. 'Please go on.'

André told them all about the tomb and its patron

goddess while Val snuggled up against Peter, smiling mischievously. The bouncing of the jeep through the hot sand had created a subtle vibration underneath her seat and she'd been squirming through most of the long drive as she felt herself growing ever damper with lust. Peter had picked up on her excitement and given her a surreptitious caress whenever her uncle wasn't looking. And as André rambled on about ancient Egyptian burial customs and funerary rites, Peter slipped a finger inside Val's sodden knickers and stroked her pussy lips. Each flick of his finger made her gasp and twitch and by the time they reached the tomb she was so aroused she could hardly walk.

They had already ascertained through carefully worded questions that there were no CCTV cameras or guards. No one to interfere with their plans, in other words. This was her uncle's find. His dig; therefore his jurisdiction. They were being let in because he had vouched for their trustworthiness.

'Well, here we are,' André said, gesturing grandly into the dusty cave entrance.

Peter shouldered their bags and peered into the darkness. 'Hmm. It's smaller than I expected.'

'And just what *did* you expect?' André asked, clearly offended. 'A lavish film set, something out of *Indiana Jones* perhaps?'

Val was quick to pacify him. 'No, no, it's perfect! It's

the real thing. That's what we want. Something authentic. Something that obviously hasn't just been knocked up in a studio.'

'Absolutely,' Peter said, nodding his approval as he looked around. 'I just meant that – well, it might be crowded with all four of us ...'

Hossam was lingering in the doorway and watching them closely. It was clear he didn't trust them.

'Yes, yes,' André said irritably. 'I know you want privacy for your – art.'

Val giggled at that. Art. Oh, if only he knew.

The tomb was no less impressive for its cosy intimacy. The walls were decorated with hieroglyphics and above the doorway was a carved figure of what Val guessed must be the goddess Nekhbet. The vulture-headed lady spread her wings out to either side as though sheltering the occupant of the room, watching over her faithful priestess for all eternity.

In the centre of the floor lay a stone sarcophagus carved with more hieroglyphics. They had no doubt once been brilliantly coloured but now the symbols had faded and the stone had crumbled away in places.

'Is she in there?' Val asked in an awed whisper.

André smiled proudly. 'She is indeed. Asleep these many thousands of years.'

Peter aimed his camera at the sarcophagus and snapped a few pictures. 'Are you going to let her out?'

'In time,' André said. 'These things must be done carefully and in stages. We're a little more respectful than the Victorians who charged in and plundered the great tombs like thieves in the night. But don't worry. I don't think you'll wake her up.'

Val grinned as he gave her an uncharacteristic wink. Maybe the old boffin had a sense of humour after all.

'Well, I'll leave you to it, then,' he said. 'Will two hours be enough time?'

'Plenty,' Peter said.

'Very well.' He looked as though he was itching to tell them – again – not to touch anything, but finally he replaced his hat and waved goodbye as he left the tomb.

They listened until they heard the jeep's engine rev and then drive away. They were alone at last.

'How awesome is this!' Val exclaimed with a little spin as she took in their surroundings.

Peter smiled and slipped his arms around her from behind. He cupped her breasts beneath her light cotton dress, squeezing them firmly. The heat outside had been phenomenal but inside the tomb it was cool. Her nipples stiffened at his touch and she leaned her head back for a kiss.

Peter obliged her, then gently pushed her away. 'We'd better get started so we have something to show for our adventure.'

Val glanced back at the doorway and listened for a

moment to make sure the jeep wasn't coming back before pulling her dress off over her head. Immediately the cool air of the tomb caressed her sweat-dappled skin and she shivered with pleasure. She folded the dress neatly and laid it on top of her bag in a corner of the room. Then she unhooked her bra and slipped her knickers off. The simple act of undressing here felt wildly transgressive, if not blasphemous. But the feeling was so erotic she didn't care. She kicked off her sandals and tiptoed, naked, over to the sarcophagus.

'Beautiful,' Peter said, admiring her body. 'Just beautiful.'

'As beautiful as Akhe– ... as her, do you think?'

'A vulture priestess?' Peter scoffed. 'How could she possibly compete?'

Val laughed but she felt a little uneasy mocking the lady in whose tomb she was standing stark naked. She glanced nervously up at the winged figure over the doorway and smiled meekly at it as if to apologise for their behaviour.

When she looked back down Peter was opening the oversized first-aid kit he'd brought with them. A flurry of anticipation ran the length of her body as she watched him take out the first roll of bandages.

'Are you ready, my dear?' he asked, giving her his most wicked smile.

She nodded, nervous and excited.

Peter crouched down and began winding the gauze

carefully around her foot, then up around her calf, then her knee, then her thigh. When he reached her pelvis he split the trailing end of the gauze down the middle, wrapped it back around her leg and tied it off. Then he grabbed another roll of bandages and started the same process on her other leg.

Val sighed at the sensual pleasure as the gauze swallowed her inch by inch. It was soft as silk against her bare skin. There was something strangely soothing in the constriction of the material tightly wound around her, both minimising and intensifying her sense of touch.

When he reached the delta of her sex again she moved her hips in a sinuous figure eight, gyrating like a belly dancer. Peter grinned and kissed the shaved mound of her sex, teasing her for a moment with his tongue before returning to the first-aid kit for another roll of bandages.

'Not yet, my sweet,' he said. He held out his hand. 'Your arm, please.'

Val gave a little moan of desire and frustration before doing as she was instructed.

All around them the figures on the wall stared with inscrutable eyes, their bodies in stylised profile, their heads cloaked in fantastic headdresses, their feet and hands sensuously bare. In one corner a woman played a harp while a jackal-headed god lay, large and imperious, above her. They were surrounded by arcane symbols, as though they had somehow tumbled inside a book written in a code they could never hope to break. Falcons and owls, ankhs and ostrich feathers, gods and goddesses whose names they didn't know. Her uncle had mentioned funerary texts. Were they prayers? An epitaph? A history? Or possibly – as her romantic and adventurous imagination couldn't help but wonder – a curse?

Peter had finished wrapping both arms, hands and each individual finger and now he was winding a new roll of gauze around her neck. He paused to give her a kiss before feeding the bandages under her arms and around her chest. When he pressed the gauze against her breasts Val gasped and writhed a little at the teasing contact. She felt her nipples tighten and she whimpered, widening her eyes pleadingly at Peter, urging him to touch her. But he remained focused and carried on with his work, manfully ignoring her entreaty as he encased her torso in bandages.

André had said that servants and pets were often mummified along with their masters and mistresses, so that they might continue to perform their duties in the afterlife. Val closed her eyes and imagined that she was the favourite slave of a powerful pharaoh. She would be wrapped like a gift for him, a plaything to take with him into the underworld. She would dance for him and pleasure him and serve him throughout all eternity.

Suddenly she felt the pressure of the gauze between her legs and she gave a little cry as Peter pulled the bandages tight up against her sex and tucked them into a strip he'd looped around her waist. He made several passes, winding the gauze tighter and tighter before tying off the end. The tension made her cunt throb with desire and the slightest movement was almost unbearably stimulating. She pressed her thighs together, flushed with heat. Her heart began to race as she realised they were nearly there.

He took her face in his hands and kissed her deeply before starting again at her neck and this time working upwards. He wound the bandage around her mouth, her upper lip, her nose. Val tried to slow her breathing and calm herself as she felt herself disappearing bit by bit. He left her eyes till last, winding the gauze over the top of her head and underneath her chin before bringing it back around the back of her head again, pulling it tight so it wouldn't come undone.

'I love you,' he whispered. Then he drew the last strip across her eyes, blindfolding her.

Val stood very still, balancing in the dark as she waited for what she knew was coming next. She relaxed as Peter gathered her in his arms and laid her down on the sarcophagus. The stone was rough and cool beneath her. She could feel both through the bandages but she could no longer feel the movement of air in the tomb.

With her ears covered, all sound was distorted. She thought she heard the harsh cry of some animal out in the desert. The rush of blood in her ears might be the currents of the Nile and the clicking of Peter's camera the beating wings of great birds soaring above the pyramids. She could make out flashes of light behind her eyes with each photo Peter took and these she imagined were the blinking eyes of the sun god, Ra. How strange that depriving her of her senses should only serve to make them more acute!

She squirmed atop the stone coffin, wondering if the lady sleeping beneath her – Akhenekhbet, that was her name! – had had a lover like hers. She was a priestess, so perhaps sex was denied to her. Did she then pleasure herself in secret and ask forgiveness of her goddess? Or did she surrender to the temptation of her beautiful handmaidens and stroke their soft wet folds, kiss their dusky pink nipples?

Val's body tingled with every stimulating thought. She flexed her feet, wriggling her bound toes. She arched her back against the unyielding stone, relishing the extreme denial of her senses.

After a while she heard a peculiar muffled sound and it took her a moment to realise that it was Peter's voice. His voice seemed to reach her telepathically. He was asking her something. No, he was asking her to *do* something. Spread her legs.

She felt herself grow warm as she obeyed, gripping the edges of the stone lid with her bandaged hands. In her mind the little slave girl obeyed too, splaying her long shapely legs for her master.

Then there was the heat and pressure of a hand between her legs, the exquisite force of a palm against her sex. A low moan escaped her as the hand pressed harder, moving in slow forceful circles. She couldn't keep from writhing. The little slave girl moved with her, grinding her pelvis as her master stroked her sex and elicited gasps and cries from her pretty lips.

Suddenly the hand was gone and Val whimpered behind the bandages. But the abandonment only lasted a moment. Soon she felt Peter's fingers untying the knot at her waist. He directed her by his touch alone to raise her hips and he slowly unwrapped the part of her he wanted to reveal. Each uncoiling of the bandages made her tremble with excitement and when her bare skin was at last exposed to the cool air her cunt pounded with need. After such constriction the tiny sensitive nerve endings were overwhelmed by stimulation.

Take me, she thought, willing him to hear her voice.

Please, master, the little slave girl begged likewise.

Peter lowered Val's bottom to the cold stone and eased her legs apart again. She shivered as the chill kissed her warm wet opening. Peter's fingers gripped her inner thighs to push them wider apart, his thumbs probing the slick folds of her pussy and spreading her lips. In her mind the slave girl whimpered submissively as her master exposed her, examined and explored her, inspected her and found her satisfactory.

43

Overwhelmed by the power of the fantasy, Val thrust her hips forwards, urging Peter to touch her, take her, fuck her.

And then he was there. She felt the smooth hard bulge of his cock at the entrance to her cunt and she pushed herself against him. Inch by slow inch, he slid himself inside. She clenched herself around him, certain she could make herself come without his help if he continued to tease her so mercilessly. Ah, but that would be cheating. An obedient slave wouldn't do such a thing. An obedient slave would wait for her master to reward her.

Peter held himself still inside her as he untied another swathe of bandages, this time the ones covering her breasts. He didn't unwind the whole length from around her body, but merely loosened them so he could peel the layers apart and expose the hard buds of her nipples. Softly, gently, he placed a fingertip on each stiff little point, exerting only the slightest pressure and moving in almost imperceptible circles.

Her body shuddered with the effort of keeping still as she surrendered to the exquisite torment. Deep inside her, his cock throbbed with his own arousal. It must have taken all his willpower to resist simply ravishing her. His weight shifted and she felt his hot breath against her right nipple. Then his lips brushed her gently. Then his tongue. She arched back against the stone, thrusting her breasts up to him like an offering. He closed his lips over each one in turn, moving his tongue back and forth over them in slow, languid strokes.

The focused stimulation was nearly unbearable. All the rest of her was still bound tightly, deprived of all sensation, while her most sensitive parts were on display, drawing all the attention.

The inner walls of her sex flexed like a hungry mouth against his cock and finally he began to fuck her in earnest, pushing himself in up to the hilt and then slowly drawing himself out. Her head tossed from side to side and she felt the bandages there begin to come loose. Seeing it, Peter took hold of the gauze and unravelled it from her head. The material fell away from her in soft coils and at first it was too bright for Val to open her eyes. She kept them closed and lay back on the stone coffin as Peter pounded in and out of her.

Now that her mouth was released from its bondage she was free to cry out and she held nothing back, not caring if she roused all the gods and goddesses from their countless millennia of sleep. She wrapped her bandaged arms and legs around Peter, missing the tactile pleasure of his warm skin against hers but luxuriating in the erotic deprivation.

When he suddenly withdrew she cried out in dismay and her eyes flew open. But a surge of lust went through her as she met his devilish smile. He eased himself up and she gazed at his naked body, burnished by the desert sun.

Without needing to say a word he pointed at the floor to one side of the sarcophagus. Val obediently slipped down from the cold stone and, although she knew what he wanted, she waited for him to position her himself.

He took her firmly by the arms and turned her around to face the sarcophagus. Her cunt was pounding like a distant drum, primal and demanding, and she grew light-headed as she imagined her slave-girl self instructed by her master to do what Peter now wanted her to do. Her legs no longer felt like they were part of her. She trembled, bracing herself against the stone until Peter pushed her down across it and peeled away the bandages covering her bottom. Her inner thighs were sticky with their combined juices and Peter swiped his fingers across her soaked pussy before smearing the wetness against the puckered little rosebud of her arse. Her face flooded with heat and she lowered her head submissively as he spread her cheeks apart and positioned himself behind her.

Her master was going to take her, fuck his obedient little slave in her most secret, intimate place, her tightest hole. For she belonged to him. She was his property and he could do as he wished with her.

It was the dirtiest game, this transgressive act. And Val gasped as his cock pushed against her, spreading her open slowly to take his length. Peter groaned with pleasure as he eased himself past the taut little ring of her anus and deep inside the tender core of her. He held her around the waist, his hands strong and forceful. He filled her completely.

She barely noticed the subtle grinding sound of stone on stone as Peter fucked her, slamming his pelvis against her buttocks with each brutal thrust. Their bodies fit together perfectly, her bottom accepting his cock and its intoxicating blend of bliss and discomfort. With every hungry stroke he reminded her that she was his. His wife, his lover, his best friend, his whore. And, in her mind, his slave.

When she felt him about to come she arched her spine and pushed back against him so he could reach around to her front. His fingers found her clit and massaged it with expert strokes. Fast and rough, just how she liked it. Her body exploded with his and she loosed a wild animal cry into the stillness of the tomb, gasping and panting with euphoric release.

Afterwards she sank blissfully to her knees and then collapsed in a heap on the dusty floor. She lay basking in the diminishing eddies of pleasure as she gazed in wonderment at the hieroglyphics around them. Her eye fell on a large carved figure of a man holding a sceptre and a flail. Before him was a kneeling woman, dressed plainly, her head bowed. It made her squirm.

'Akhenekhbet,' she whispered, blushing. 'Thank you.'

'What was that?'

Val smiled as Peter helped her to her feet. 'Oh, nothing. Just thanking our hostess for a lovely time.'

'Mmmm,' he said. He blew a kiss to the sarcophagus. '*Shukran.*'

'And what was *that*?'

'Well, I hope it was "thank you". I left the phrasebook at the hotel.'

'Oh shit!'

'It's not a big deal, Val,' he laughed. 'Your uncle can speak to Hossam –'

'No. Look.'

Peter looked where she was pointing and gasped. Their violent passion had dislodged the lid of the sarcophagus. Only slightly, but enough to be noticed. Worse still, try as they might, they couldn't push it back into place.

Val grinned sheepishly. 'I guess we'll just have to say we bumped it or something. Come on, our two hours are almost up and you've got to unwrap me.'

Normally they would have savoured the process, drawing it out and exploiting the hypersensitivity of Val's newly unbound flesh. But André and his assistant would be back at any moment.

Peter began stuffing the sprawling lengths of bandages into a carrier bag but Val stopped him. 'Wait. I've got an idea.' Her eyes sparkled with mischief.

* * *

The jeep bumped to a dusty halt outside the entrance to the tomb. Peter and Val were waiting outside.

Val kissed her uncle as he and Hossam approached. 'We were just enjoying the night sky.'

'Yes, it's lovely, isn't it?' André said genially. 'Did you get all you needed?'

'I think so,' Peter said. 'There's definitely some unique material here.' He patted his camera bag.

'Well, I suppose we should get you back to your hotel. You'll want to wash off all that dust.'

Peter and Val shared a playful grin before the desert night was shattered by a scream. It had come from inside the tomb. All three froze for a moment and then Hossam emerged shakily from the entrance, repeating something over and over in Arabic and staring wildly into the darkness around them. In his hand he held a torn strip of gauze.

André's eyes widened in horror.

'What's he saying?' Peter asked.

For a moment André was too stunned to answer. When he spoke at last his voice was a guttural croak. 'He said … "She walks".'

The Big Gift
Valerie Grey

I wanted a big cock in me, a really huge monster cock that would stretch my pussy like I was giving birth. Why? Because I had never been fucked by a man who was hung like a Nephilim, and I was intensely, obsessively curious what it would be like. I had just turned thirty-one; I had had sex with only three men in my life, two average-size and one very small. My husband, Gregory, is one of the average guys at six inches.

For my thirty-first birthday, Gregory treated me to a night of dinner and dancing. It was nice, as it always is nice, each year of our seven years of marriage. My husband is like an old reliable car: never any surprises, always dependable.

We want for nothing – nothing material, that is. That's not to say we're filthy rich and have a Beverly Hills mansion or an apartment in The Dakota; but we live comfortably in a clean, upper-class neighbourhood.

So why did I feel there was something missing?

You can say there was a hole in me that needed to be filled – a big hole that needed something enormous to fill it.

* * *

When I was a child my mother religiously made a daily entry in her diary. She always told me her personal history was important to her, that it was a form of anthropology she called auto-ethnography. She found satisfaction in reading and recalling her past, especially her spirited youth, lovers won and lost and the many blessings received by having children.

I followed her advice. I've been keeping a diary since I was twelve years old. It was that diary that caused things to change in my comfortable married life.

I don't know if I left the diary out in the open consciously or I simply forgot to put it away; maybe my subconscious devious self *wanted* him to read it. My husband knew I valued my privacy and, as far as I knew, had never violated that trust by reading my secret thoughts, but he saw the diary and his natural curiosity threw respect out the window. He only read my most recent entry but it was enough to hurt him deeply. It took him several weeks to admit it to me; what he read disturbed him so much he *had* to talk about it.

51

The entry read: 'There are moments, like today, when a restlessness wells up inside of me. A time when I want to know what it would feel like to be filled like a slut. To have my womb tickled by the head of a very huge cock, my imaginary G-spot probed like an alien abductee's, my total cunt cavity filled to capacity, stretched to impossibility so that my whole being, the universe, was that cock tearing me apart with forceful thrusts, ravished and pillaged like women in romance novels are raped by Fabio. I wonder if Fabio has a big dick? You'd be surprised but sometimes the most attractive men and the sexy alpha male womanisers are lacking in that department, as if attempting to compensate for missing girth or dimension.

'That was the case with my second boyfriend, a desirable fellow all the girls wanted, a star athlete in football and water polo, who dressed like a *GQ* model and drove a sports car. How did I get so lucky? I wondered. But when the time came, he had a tiny penis, thin like a pencil; it felt like a finger inside me instead of a penis. He cried and said he was sorry. I told him size didn't matter and I believed that at first and later knew it was a lie.

'I was glad that Gregory's penis was not that small, the first time I went to bed with him, which was on a respectable third date ... but I was also a tad disappointed because he wasn't big. I was curious to know what it would be like with a man whose penis was so big it could not fit in and who hurt me just by sticking the head inside me. Some women I know say they fear long or thick cocks, and others say the pain is actually wonderful and you soon stretch out so you can take it. I guess I will never know that feeling, a feeling I think about all the time, a fulfilling I yearn for the way a caged animal looks out at an open field and imagines what freedom feels like.'

You can see how this would concern a husband who thought everything was hunky-dory in his marriage – and our marriage was fine as far as I was concerned. Only when these occasional longings arose did I question my sexual fulfilment, and when these depraved thoughts tortured me I could usually eradicate them by masturbating for an hour or two. I enjoyed these rare times because it always required multiple orgasms, and I'm talking ten to fifteen of the little fuckers.

Now this particular entry in my diary could be interpreted as an insult to my husband's manhood. I can only imagine the agony my careless words must have caused him. When he finally gathered the courage to confront me, I could see the pain and confusion in his eyes.

My immediate reaction was anger, and I almost yelled at him for invading my privacy; but then, instead, my heart ached for him. He stood before me like a beaten man.

Gregory is a gentle man, a man with a big heart (and no, not a dick that matched), a devoted husband and father. His love for me is unquestionable. But now I felt I was put in a position to prove that love. Not because I had done anything wrong; because I had a character flaw. It took most of the night to finally convince Gregory of my love for him and my happiness in our marriage. He wanted to know if all women had thoughts like those he had read. I had no idea and told him so; it just wasn't something my female friends would consider discussing. He pointed out that men talk about sex a lot, usually lying about the conquests they've made, and lying about the size of their dicks when hard and full of blood and lust.

I thought that was the end of our problem; that our all-night discussion laid it to rest. We even made love that morning before Gregory went to work. He appeared to have his manhood back, intact, six inches of macho pumping. He had a spring in his step when he left for work.

* * *

In December, Gregory came home from work with a big surprise: two airline tickets, first class, and reservations at the Luxor in Las Vegas. I was totally thrilled. He knew how I loved Vegas, how I enjoyed playing the slot machines and losing money. He said it was an early Christmas gift.

The first night we took in a Penn and Teller show and dined till we were absolutely stuffed, and I pulled on slot machines till my arms ached. The next day we slept, lounged around the pool and just did nothing. About 8 p.m., Gregory suggested we should go dancing. He loves to dance. I put on my most alluring dress, something to show all my assets. We danced away. Gregory said he spotted someone he had met earlier in the day. He excused himself and went to the bar to talk to this someone; in a few minutes he was back with a young man wearing a Santa Claus cap and introduced him as Lance, a resident of Nevada. Gregory insisted I dance with Lance, who was taller than Gregory, perhaps six foot three, with broad shoulders, a small waist and a butt any woman or girl would die for. 'Extremely' handsome fits the description – one of those men who are too good looking, if that's possible, because such attractiveness often means bad-boy trouble. Not that I knew this for certain, recalling my second boyfriend, who was also extremely handsome but barely had a penis.

As we danced he complimented me on my dress and the way I moved my body, how my hair smelled – everything a woman wants to hear. I could feel his eyes and hands all over my body and it seemed like he deliberately pressed his manhood against my abdomen. Such touch was not lost on me, for I could feel that he was not normal – *huge* might be the word to describe it. I swear

I felt it grow and I experienced a rush of excitement, of embarrassment, as we ground against one another in a manner that at any other time, in any other place or setting, I would find disturbing if not disgusting.

We left the dancefloor and Gregory said he had a headache and was going back to the room. I nodded OK; Lance was making me nervous and I wanted to get away from what could only amount to trouble. Gregory insisted I stay with Lance and have a good time dancing; I mean he really insisted and so did Lance. This was so uncharacteristic of my husband. I asked Lance to excuse us for a minute and took Gregory aside. I wanted to know what he was doing, leaving me with a total stranger. He explained to me he had found Lance on the internet and this was his gift of love. I didn't immediately understand. He reminded me of my diary; this was his way of letting me live out my fantasy. Lance was a gigolo from a service, and his speciality was … size. Gregory said he had seen a photo of Lance's tool of the trade, as it were, and he was a good thirteen inches long and four inches wide.

I was totally stunned. I was flabbergasted and appalled. I was intrigued and aroused. I tried to explain to him that I couldn't do something like this; I couldn't go off with a complete stranger and have sex; I was a married woman, etc. Gregory was adamant, saying he had already paid for the 'service' and it cost quite a bit and he knew this is what I wanted deep inside and I should be happy to have such a husband. He pushed me back towards Lance and walked away.

What man would do this for his wife or, for that matter, *to* his wife?

* * *

I was uncomfortable as I sat down next to Lance at a table. It was awkward, to say the least. I was uneasy but, I must admit, curious. After a few drinks and several dances, I loosened up considerably, feeling myself wet from the closeness of Lance's obvious giant manhood. There was a knot developing in my stomach in anticipation of what might happen.

I told him I knew who and what he was; that he had been hired to fulfil my secret dark fantasy. He smiled and suggested we go to his room so I could have my gift at last. I couldn't speak. He took my hand and led me to the elevator. He had a small room, a single with a queen-size bed. There was a fully stocked wet bar. He made two vodka tonics. As we sipped our drinks he began nibbling my ear, licking inside, and I became jelly.

Weakly, I asked him, 'Do you really have a big penis?'

He smiled and stood in front of me, his belt buckle staring me in the eye. 'Find out for yourself,' he said.

I quickly undid the belt, zipped down his trousers and let them fall to the floor, and there it was, three inches from my face: a freak of nature, an appendage so large it took my breath away. His bikini briefs couldn't contain it and it wasn't even hard yet. I pulled the penis out of his briefs and held the head up – an enormous bulb, an impossibility of man flesh. I could barely get it in my mouth; my jaw muscles ached trying to hold my lips open around it. As I slowly sucked on what I could, it began to grow. I thought the corners of my mouth would split and I envied snakes for not having jawbones, able to swallow creatures of any size. I removed Lance's penis quickly, fearing it would harm me. I licked it, the full length; I could not get my fingers around it.

He grabbed my hair and told me to lick his balls, which were also huge and sagging and hairy and musty. I licked them, tried to get one testicle in my mouth the way Gregory likes me to do, and it was a task. I looked up at Lance's face, his blue, penetrating eyes glaring down at me as if he were a hawk and I was prey. I blubbered something about it being too large, that I didn't think any woman could take a cock this huge. He laughed and told me that not all women could, but some could, and that any bold woman had to at least try. There was no way I was leaving without trying, he informed me. 'This is what you have wanted for a long time,' he said. And he was so right, so very, *very right*.

I stood and turned, and he unzipped me out of my dress. He forced me down on the bed. I spread myself submissively, giving in and accepting whatever would happen: if he killed me with his cock, so be it. He lay down next to me, kissed my cheeks and stroked my bare tits. My nipples were sensitive and exquisitely painful to his touch. He leaned over to the nightstand and retrieved a bottle of lubricant. He handed it to me and, without a word, I began smearing it all over his monster cock. I was in such awe; I had imagined this moment many times, had masturbated to it, but I never knew what it truly would be like to have a monster cock in my hands, the thick veins pulsating like something from a sci-fi movie.

He moved above me; I instinctively grasped his penis and placed the head against my pussy lips. I was having misgivings. I thought there was no way this could ever happen, I could never handle it, might as well try to get an elephant to penetrate a mouse. He pushed slowly, the head stretching me to new dimensions, so wide I knew I would split. The pain, however, was a good pain, a pain I could stand. I spread my legs more for maximum room. Two inches, three inches, four. My hips thrust upwards – five, six, and that was only half his cock. I felt absolutely primitive, sucking this huge piece of meat up into my very core. I knew the orgasm building in me would make me forget all the other orgasms I had ever had or would have. This was going to be *the one*, the one I had fantasised so many times.

And then it happened: I had no control of my body. I convulsed, screamed, whimpered and cried as wave after wave of pleasure washed over me like a tsunami taking out islands. I had never experienced such a moment: both the cock filling me and the orgasm dominating me. Lance's thrusting never lost stride; he continued to fuck me, and fuck me, and fuck me. I lost count – stopped counting as I came, came and came again over the course of two hours of pure wild fucking. This gigolo had stamina; he was a professional at this, and probably in demand, with so many women to pleasure in Las Vegas, so many women in need of big lust.

He stopped, his penis still buried deep inside me. His staying power was godlike, I thought, and I wondered if he would ever come. I was tired and closed my eyes for a moment and fell asleep. I was awakened by Lance's continuing, thrusting tempo and my own hips meeting his, slamming that huge piece of fuck flesh in and out of me. So we were at it again. I knew my pussy lips were raw from this continuous fuck. Very soon – I couldn't believe it – I was climaxing again. Just when I thought I would beg him to stop, another wave of that torturing pleasure would overtake me. My hands were clasping his taut ass cheeks and, for the first time, I felt their clenching muscles begin to flinch. He was going to shoot inside me and only then did I realise that I was having intercourse without any method of safety. Then again, would a Magnum condom even fit on him? I doubted it. I was here, we had been fucking for nearly three straight hours with just one small break, I had no idea how many orgasms I'd had and now, finally, this male prostitute was going to have his. I wanted it. I felt his cock throbbing inside me as his hot semen filled and warmed my womb.

I was exhausted.

Lance rolled off of me and went into the bathroom. By the time he returned I was dressed. He didn't understand and showed his displeasure. He had planned on resting a while and continuing our fucking spree. 'I've been paid for the night,' he said.

I apologised profusely, trying to make him understand that this was the best sex I had ever had in my life. But I also had a husband who allowed me this experience and I didn't want him to worry. He nodded and said he understood but, if I changed my mind, I could return to his room any time tonight.

I walked down the hall to the elevator and my legs were so wobbly, I thought I would fall. My entire body was sore and battered like a whipped slave, and my vagina ... my pussy was raw and aching. I could feel I was gaping down there, widened by Lance's monster meat, and wondered if I would return to normal, if Lance had ruined me and my pussy would be too loose for my husband.

In the elevator, I felt a gush of semen pour out of me and run down my leg. I was loose all right.

* * *

Gregory was watching television. It was three in the morning. I knew he wouldn't be sleeping. He was watching the hotel's porno channel. I knew he had been masturbating. His eyes searched for any difference in me. His curiosity got the better of him and he began pummelling me with questions. I was so tired I wanted to wait till later; I wanted to think about my answers, afraid I might say something that could hurt him.

I went to the bathroom to clean the splooge off my leg and around my pussy. My lips looked abused and red. It hurt to clean them. I sat on the toilet and out gushed another river of come.

I undressed and crawled into bed. Gregory lay next to me, still asking me what it was like, was it what I had always wanted, was I happy, did he make me come? How would he react if I told him the gigolo gave me more orgasms in three hours than I'd probably had all my life? How would he feel if I told him that Lance's cock was like taking a redwood tree up my cunt? I kissed my husband on the cheek, told him I appreciated his gesture in allowing me to fulfil my fantasy but I had to sleep. I turned, buried my head in the soft pillow, I felt

Lance's come juice leaking from my pussy ... vulgarly running down my leg.

Gregory woke me at noon. I staggered into the bathroom; my body seemed to reek of stale sex and it aroused me. I jumped into the shower, where the hot water caressed my aching muscles. But it hurt my vagina and I still felt gaping wide and really began to worry that I had been ruined by that hired cock.

I put on a thin dress, knowing that slacks or jeans would rub against my sore sex and would hurt. I was relieved that Gregory didn't start in on me again about my experience. We went down to the hotel dining room for brunch and I spotted Lance sitting on the far side of the room, alone. Gregory did not see him. Lance gave me a look and he stood up and walked down a hallway to the restrooms. I told Gregory I needed to pee and quickly followed Lance.

* * *

He was waiting for me. He grabbed me firmly by the arm and led me to the men's room door. He pushed it open with his leg and in a loud voice enquired if anyone was in there. No answer. He pulled me in and locked the door.

Why was he acting like a brute alpha male, taking me like a CroMagnon would? I told him I only wanted to thank him for the nice night but we both knew that was a lie. I tried to pull away but, being so strong, he turned me around and forced me to face the large mirror. I leaned against the counter and watched in the mirror as he unzipped his trousers and pulled his fuck beast out. It looked bigger than I remembered. The giant dick nudged me from behind and he ordered me to spread my legs.

'Think you could take it in the ass?' he whispered angrily into my ear.

My face turned pale. I didn't know what to say. I couldn't even take my husband's cock in the ass, and I never cared that much for anal.

Lance laughed. 'Don't worry, I won't split your bum,' he said. What had gotten into him? Last night he was the seductive gentle lover, and now he was a crass aggressive bastard. He pulled my panties down, almost ripped them. I felt the experienced fingers on my cunt and I flinched. Despite the pain, within seconds I was soaking wet and then the bulb of his cock was inside me. My eyes widened and I told him I was too bruised and sore for sex but he did not seem to care. This was not his finest hour. I listened to him grunt, apparently with only one thing in mind, to please himself and only himself. I no longer mattered. I remembered he had been paid for the night; now it was morning and he did not have to act like the gentleman gigolo ... now he was a free agent and I was his conquest, not a client.

'Stretch that dirty cunt and take it,' he growled. 'Take it, you cock-loving whore!'

I was thrilled to be roughly fucked in this vulgar, brusque manner. My ass was pushing backwards, begging for him to bury his meat in me; the hell with pain, I would take the pain with the guilty pleasure. He obliged by fucking me vigorously. Within minutes we both came, our bodies convulsed and shuddered in one intense orgasm. I was surprised how sweaty I had become from this quick sexual encounter. Last night he had lasted for three hours; this morning it was three minutes.

He turned me around, grasped my shoulders and forced me to kneel down and clean him with my mouth. As I knelt, legs spread, I could feel his come running out of me into a puddle on the floor. I licked his cock, from head to base, slurping up my juices mixed with spunk.

'Merry Christmas,' he said, and left.

I had never been treated in such a manner and the act turned me on in a way that frightened me. Last night Lance had treated me like a queen and now he was turning me into a dirty slut. I felt dirty and used – and sexy.

* * *

I quickly went into the women's restroom and tried to clean myself before returning to Gregory, washing my face and crotch with paper towels. There was nothing

I could do about my breath. As I walked through the dining room, I was certain everyone I passed could surely smell it on me: the sex, the sperm. Maybe I imagined it, because Gregory didn't seem to smell anything, or acted like he didn't. He said Lance happened to stop by the table and told Gregory I was one of the best sex clients he had ever had. 'I think he was hoping for a tip,' my husband added with a laugh. 'I don't know, should I have slipped him an extra $100 for fucking my wife good?'

I didn't say that Lance had collected his tip just a few minutes ago.

'I want to know,' Gregory said after we ate. With food and Lance's come nestled in my belly, I told my husband about his extraordinary holiday gift to me.

Layover
Jeremy Edwards

Dear Amy,

You had just asked me about my vacation when my phone died on us last night. Apologies! But in a way I'm glad the technology failed us at that juncture, because although I did indeed want to tell you about my vacation, the part I especially wanted to relate would not lend itself to a phone conversation.

You know that I never tire of hearing your cheerful voice. But we also used to correspond quite a bit, didn't we? And no doubt you recall how for a while after our 'amicable breakup' we honoured a sort of unspoken pact to entertain each other with accounts of our respective sexual adventures. Remember? I'm not sure when or how we got out of that habit, but I miss it. And I hope you might welcome this e-mail as an attempt to revive the tradition. But even if that's not to be – even if this is a one-off – it's important to me to share this story with you. I'm not entirely sure why, but maybe you'll have an insight.

You're probably aware of my 'thing' for flight attendants. Yes, yes, this predictable guy has a predictable turn-on. If you were here, I'm sure you'd tease me about it. I'd enjoy that.

But, speaking seriously, this passion is something I've always felt with my heart. I have tender feelings for the airline women that I masturbate about. The real ones, the imaginary ones. I even kiss them goodnight at the end of the fantasies. Don't laugh.

When most men say female flight attendants are 'hot', it's more of a knee-jerk reaction, don't you think? You know what I mean: men's magazines and old movies and all that. But here's the twist: flight attendants really are sexy, sexy as hell. It's something about their competence and – what would you call it? – maybe *flexibility*. There's a kind of nobility to them. And most guys are completely missing it. It's as if they're so focused on the frosting they don't realise there's a cake.

I've seen these guys when I fly, eating up a professional smile like it's all for them. Personally, I would never be so presumptuous. That smile's not for me – not for me in particular, I mean. That smile is a woman doing a job.

But after she's served me my tomato juice and moved on, I imagine that I can hear her heartbeat and smell her pussy – and I wish I could make her feel wonderful all over.

What makes me especially horny, Amy, is when they go rolling off to their hotels. There's always a little group of them, the men and the women, in those dark coats. I watch the women – from a polite distance, of course – as they traipse out of the airport, their shoes click-clacking all the way. Their faces always look tired ... tired but relaxed, now that they've clocked out. Often the whole bunch of them are laughing together. They're chummy. *Intimate.* So, yes, I watch them, hoping that, after a lot more laughter and a couple of drinks, every one of those women will get fucked to her heart's content in the layover suite. The men as well, of course, but that's not my department.

In my fantasies, I'm magically included in these little layover parties, from cocktails all the way to that goodnight kiss I mentioned. In the fantasies, by the way, I'm the one pouring the booze. The airline women are off duty now; it's their turn to be taken care of.

Let's face it: hotels are erotic to begin with. Large or small, what you're getting from a hotel boils down to a room with a bed. Now, in my experience a bed is for two things. It's like the hotel is saying to you, here's a place for you to sleep and fuck, and not necessarily in that order. It makes me feel that the room is full of fuck, even when I'm the only one in it.

Now let me tell you what happened on my way back from visiting little sister Kimmy down south.

I was waiting for a connecting flight out of Philadelphia. The terminal was crowded with evening departures, but nothing seemed to be moving. Finally they admitted their computers had gone down. They were going to have to cancel all their flights for the rest of the day.

Some people got shifted over to other airlines. Some, if they lived in Philly or had stayed with someone there, called their people to come get them. As for the rest of us ... well, there was no way the airline could weasel out of responsibility. So they got busy arranging accommodation, at their expense.

When I saw some of the other passengers board a shuttle bus with a group of airline personnel, I felt a tad jealous. Childish, I know. As it happened, I was the last one left waiting for a different bus to a different hotel. Or I thought I was. Just as my bus pulled up, a woman in flight-attendant gear joined me at the kerb. She was a redhead about your height, a little younger than I am. She had kind eyes, like most of them.

She smiled. 'I guess it's just the two of us going to Rittenhouse Square.'

'Rittenhouse Square?' I know my way around Philly, Amy. If the airline was sending us to *that* neighbourhood, this had to be some fancy hotel.

'Yep, that's where they're putting us up. Can you believe it? Everything else is full.'

I asked her why she wasn't with the rest of the crew.

'Oh, I'm the spillover,' she explained as we boarded.

'Me, too, I guess.'

'If I'd known I was going to be sleeping in luxury, I'd have brought a fancy nightgown,' she said. 'Or, better yet, a fancy man.' We had taken our seats in the back of the otherwise empty bus by the time she said this. She followed it up with a wink.

I didn't know how to react. She was playing right to my turn-on – but she couldn't have known that, and I didn't want to say anything stupid. So I just smiled, and after looking at me for a second or two she laughed, as if to say it was OK that I didn't reply – that I seemed like a friendly enough guy, and all was cool. I spent the rest of the bus ride imagining her half out of her uniform in a big hotel bed with some attentive, lucky companion.

At the check-in counter of this palace they'd sent us to, they were surprised, just as I'd been, that Margie wasn't with other crew. In fact, there was some kind of mix-up and they'd reserved a big suite for her, thinking she was a party of three. For me, they'd opened up a convertible couch in a small conference room.

Though our accommodations were very different, they were on the same floor. Margie rolled her suit-case alongside me as we headed over to the eleva-tors. I noted the absence of the familiar click-clack of shoes, courtesy of the plush hotel carpeting. I instinctively looked at her feet. I wondered if she had bedroom slippers in her bag.

Her room – or rather her *suite* – was on the way to mine. I nodded goodnight. Then, while I was figuring out whether the conference room was straight ahead or around the corner, I heard her door open again.

'Wow. You have to check this out, Lenny,' she said. I'd told her my name was Leonard, so she was calling me Lenny – even though, as you know, nobody does.

You understand the situation, right? This was the biggest, fanciest hotel room you could imagine, and she wanted to show it to me. Because it had been only the two of us on that bus, and I was sort of her buddy for this excursion into luxury. I dared not assume anything further.

But there I was, in a flight attendant's hotel room – and the realisation hit me like a ton of bricks. There was her suitcase right on the luggage stand, open and everything. She must have unzipped it as soon as she set it down there, before coming to get me. I suppose if you're a flight attendant, you're efficient that way. But the open suitcase made me feel as if I were seeing her with her panties down.

I set my bag on the floor, as well as my raincoat, and we toured the elegant suite – the foyer, the living room, the two bedrooms, the kitchenette, the *two* bathrooms.

'I wish I could throw a party in this place,' Margie said.

It was then we noticed the whisky bottle on top of the minibar. It was strange, because there was the usual pay-to-play booze fridge, but this lone bottle was out, free and clear – a full bottle of Scotch, never opened. Good stuff, too. Someone must have forgotten it.

She picked up the bottle. 'Want to have a party, Lenny?'

She didn't wait for me to answer – she was already grabbing a couple of glasses. But if I was going to do this, I had to do it right. 'Allow me,' I said, or something to that effect. And I poured her a drink, along with one for myself.

She clinked my glass. 'Here's to the spillover,' she said.

Yes, that was cute as hell, but I could barely pay attention to the conversation. My head was already spinning from the whole scenario – I hadn't had a sip yet, mind you – and nothing seemed real.

Margie kicked her shoes off and sat on a sofa near the minibar. Her feet looked tired – limp – but beautiful. Noble little feet, still in stockings.

'You must miss your friends,' I said. It was undoubtedly a silly remark, but I was thinking how normally they'd all be together, doing who knows what between flights.

'Nah,' she said. 'Not really.'

'No?'

'I get to spend plenty of layover evenings with them. I've never spent one with you before, Lenny.' She raised her glass, as if toasting me.

'I've never had one,' I said awkwardly. 'A layover with … airline people. I always wondered what you folks did.' That seemed the tasteful way to put it.

She looked at me sweetly, as if she thought perhaps I was a bit pathetic but she liked me anyway. She put the drink down, stood up and walked towards me.

'What do we do? We have little parties. Just like this.'

She stepped closer.

'We have parties –' she was touching my chest now '– and we. Have. Sex.' She said it as three separate sentences, the way people do when they wish to make a point. She poked my chest for each sentence.

I put my drink down now, too.

Margie kept talking, which was a relief to me since I was rather overwhelmed and tongue-tied. 'Is that what you've always wondered about, Lenny? About the sex? Because I could tell you allllll about the sex.'

But instead of telling me 'allllll' about the sex, she moved her hand down to my trousers. She could feel my hard-on and she kept her hand there, caressing me through the cloth.

'Would you like me to suck your big hard dick, Lenny?'

And this was where I began to feel less tongue-tied. You see, she'd thrown me a cue that made it easier to express myself. 'You can do that if you want, Margie,' I said. 'But what I really want is whatever makes *you* feel the best.' After all, this, to me, was the whole point of being stranded in Philadelphia with a flight attendant.

I stood there looking at her face, wondering what her desires were. If sucking my dick was what she would get off on, then you wouldn't catch me complaining. But first things first: I wanted desperately to hear her tell me what she desired most.

She stroked me with a bit more oomph. Maybe it turned her on for me to ask what she wanted. It certainly turned *me* on. Consider: a lovely woman works her pretty ass off in a plane all day ... and then *yours truly* gets to hand her the pleasure menu? I felt impossibly fortunate.

'What a thoughtful man you are,' she said, still rubbing me. I smiled and said that was no problem at all, but she still hadn't answered the question. I believe I wagged my finger at her, reproaching her playfully.

I kept looking at her eyes, her kind eyes. They were green, and they looked ... hopeful, like she was expecting to enjoy herself with me. She was grinning, too. And she was still squeezing my dick; I was dancing in the palm of her hand.

'Well,' she said, 'since you insist on coaxing it out of me ... I do like sucking dick, but what I think I would like most of all tonight would be if you took my panties off. Then I could lie on that nice big bed in there, where there's plenty of space to spread my legs. I'd make room for you between my thighs, Lenny. My panties would be allllll the way out here on the floor, so it would be easy for you to touch me ... everywhere. I'd spread myself open for your thick, strong fingers ... and your sweet, generous lips ... and this handsome cock.' She gave it an extra-emphatic squeeze.

Now, you may have noticed that what she was asking for was fairly standard. But the way she said it made it feel special: she made me feel in that moment as if I'd never had the privilege of going between a woman's legs before – no offence, Amy. And I can't help thinking it's the flight-attendant thing. Am I wrong, or do they have a way of making things magical? Like when they serve you a few ounces of tomato juice in a plastic cup, but it feels like a birthday present.

She let go of my cock – she probably realised I was going to come if she didn't – and moved my hands to her hips, as though she meant to give me a dance lesson. But I didn't require a lesson for this.

Her hips were deliciously solid – with a beautiful curve to them – and I ran my hands up and down the sides of the skirt. It was softer than I expected, this flight-attendant fabric. It tickled my fingertips.

Then I just had to feel around the back of the skirt. I can't tell you how many times I'd imagined myself sampling the feel of an airline woman's ass through one of those skirts. This was my chance to find out what it was really like.

So how did it feel? Womanly. Comforting. Even though I was the one fondling her, it was like her bottom was caressing me instead. And I was thinking about how this tickly fabric probably felt very pleasant on her skin, on the places the panties didn't reach. So I kept stroking her soft ass awhile, through the skirt.

Eventually I reached up under the skirt, as smoothly as I could, and ran my hands over her panties, particularly in the front. They were satin, and I could feel her bush when I pressed against them. She shifted her thighs when I touched her there. She made little feminine sounds, looking right at me so I could see the expression on her face.

I said 'smoothly', but I admit I was practically shaking, I was so turned on. But I took hold of the panties and rolled them down, without displacing the skirt. She did a shimmy to make them fall down her legs, then she took my hand. She left the panties lying right there on the floor, as she'd said she would. They were white, to complement the navy-blue uniform.

'I have to pee, Lenny,' Margie informed me with a giggle. 'Come on and help me choose which bathroom to use.'

She didn't really need much help choosing – the closer of the two bathrooms seemed to suit her fine – but she appeared to want the company. She pulled me towards the toilet as she plunked herself prettily down, keeping hold of my hand while she manoeuvred her skirt with an efficient one-handed grace that testified to countless quick pees in cramped airplane facilities. She kept the short skirt more or less in place over her lap, so the view I got was suggestive but not explicit.

She freed the toilet paper from its guest-welcoming, superfluous origami fold – also with one hand – before relaxing into the pleasure of release. She winked at me as the softly melodious trickle began, then used her free hand to grasp my trouser front and once again stroke my dick, which had thickened further under the spell of her flirty bathroom demeanour.

When she was done, she led me to the master bedroom without a word. Her body bounced when she flopped onto the bed, and she let out a big sigh – almost a moan – as if to express that she couldn't believe how good it felt to be on her back on a huge, comfy hotel mattress. She was looking up at the ceiling – looking content, almost satisfied, even though we'd barely started. Her face looked pink; it may have been the drink, though she'd hardly touched it. Or perhaps it was the way the room was lit.

And there were her strong, shapely legs, spread apart for me. Her stockings rose beyond the hem of the skirt – but with her legs wide open I could see her bare thighs above the stocking tops, and the terrain beyond. Her bush showed itself as nice and thick, though I could see only part of it. It was a shade darker red than the hair up top.

I stopped only to take my shoes off. I was dressed casually in a sweater and cords, and I didn't mind hopping on the bed just like that. For that matter, Margie was still wearing everything but shoes and panties. Even the delicious blazer, and her official airline scarf – which was obviously fine with me, given my tastes.

I started out by kissing the tops of her thighs. Her skin was milky sweet, and I could taste a smidgen of perspiration – which, as I think you know, I enjoy very much on a woman. I think she must have dabbed some perfume there, but mostly it was her natural scent that I detected. My face was so close to her pussy, I was taking her in with every breath.

Margie had mentioned my fingers, and I hadn't forgotten. She was already moist, and it was making her hair curl there, where the fur dipped down and under. I stroked the hair first, then the lips. This made the lips separate more, and my finger went in. It was so wet inside her, Amy.

I wanted to taste that, but first I had to give her my digit's worth, to make sure she knew she had a visitor. I was thorough, touching every place I could reach, and soon she was pretty worked up, moving herself frantically around my finger.

Then I pulled my finger out and went in with my face. I moved my fingers to her ass crack, and she wiggled when I did that. I began lapping her up – licking her up and down, smacking my lips against her lips, running my tongue everywhere ... slowly up to her clitty, then down almost all the way to her other hole.

'Wiggling' was no longer the right word: after a few minutes of my oral attentions, she was grinding like she meant business. I grabbed her sturdy, round ass cheeks to anchor her and I kept going, naturally. All I could think about was how I had a flight attendant's pussy in my face, and I wasn't going to stop licking until the pleasure between her legs was everything those green eyes were looking for. I was in heaven with this assignment.

It didn't take long. Margie came grandly, and her body made no secret of it. Her pussy smooched my face, if you will. There was hot woman juice all over me. The lips were twitching, the hair down there soaking wet. I kept licking her button, just to make sure she got every last sizzle. It was sticking out so seductively that I ended up sucking on it till she finished.

After that, she fucked me gently – rocking me in her arms, with my cock clasped tight in her warm, slippery pussy. She was breathing intimately into my ear the whole time. We were both still dressed, but we were naked together where it counted, apart from the condom. I did get a couple of her blouse buttons open, as well as the bra – I thought she might like it if I kissed her nipples while we fucked.

For the most part, I just let her pump me, instead of the other way around. I was happy, but over-whelmed. Excited though I was, I sort of floated, letting myself ride on the sex until I was simply coming.

She clutched me more tightly when I came, and initiated a churning motion under me to get herself off again. It was quite athletic – impressive muscle work. She whimpered when she came the second time, and she licked my earlobe. Then she leaned back flat on the mattress, like she had at the beginning. Looking up at the ceiling. Content.

And so a fantasy comes true, eh? And yet it was different somehow. For one thing, it was *quieter*: in my fantasies, everything's big and loud. Flight attendants laughing all over the place, like they've never stopped since getting off the plane. There's music, too, in the fantasies, now that I think about it. I don't know what, just something lively in the background. And – it's a tiny thing – I always see glittery ice cubes in the drinks when I fantasise, like in a magazine ad. Margie and I had our Scotch straight.

You see, this was the biggest hotel room ever, ridiculously glamorous ... but aside from Margie's vigorous orgasms, we went about everything softly, as if on tiptoes the whole time. But it was perfect this way.

Just Margie and I, on tiptoe.

I think you'll understand.

Anyway, I'll try to call you back tonight. Kimmy asked after you and told me some funny things about her new job that you'll appreciate. I look forward to picking up the thread – sorry again about the abrupt end to our talk yesterday.

And Amy: don't hesitate to write and share.

Love,

Leonard

Caribbean Heat
Kathleen Tudor

'I'm not a maid,' I said, trying to sound firm.

'Come on, Ally, I'm *dying*!' Martha did look completely pathetic curled up in the little infirmary bed. She'd taken crew leave in Tampa and come away with a nasty flu or something.

'You're not dying,' I said, but she saw in my face that she'd won me over and a wan smile lit up her brown eyes.

'I'll owe you,' she promised. I sighed and took her shift list from her. I'd trained as a maid six years ago when I'd first come aboard the *Caribbean Pearl*, but I'd worked my way up to a Guest Services position two years ago and I did not miss scrubbing toilets.

'You do owe me.' I pulled a face to let her know I wasn't really upset – well, not very, anyway – and checked the scheduled shifts. 'I can do today and tomorrow, probably. Any more than that and I'm going to get into trouble. OK?'

'I'm sure I'll be up by then. Thank you, thank you, thank you!' She finished with a coughing fit that left both of us wincing.

'OK, rest up.'

I'd have to hurry if I was going to pull this off for today. I started with the cleaning. I figured I had time to do one hall before I had to appear on deck and do a midday guest satisfaction assessment.

The head of housekeeping glared at me when I told her I needed to take out one of her carts, but I only smiled. 'Pretend I'm Martha,' I said, and her eyes softened. Martha had been dealing with a string of bad luck lately, and it had led to more time off than management liked. Her job hung by a string, and one legitimate bout of flu could cut the well-liked maid loose next time we made port in Tampa. Unless she could convince some poor idiot to cover for her, that is.

'Hurry up, then, and you be careful with my cart.' Catherine shooed me out, and I hurried to the first of Martha's assigned rooms to make beds and replace towels and, yes, scrub toilets. It was tedious, but I quickly fell back into the rhythm I was used to – almost too quickly for my comfort – and finished the last room in the corridor with a little time to spare.

I returned the cart and marked off the rooms I'd cleaned, leaving Catherine with a promise to be back as soon as I could to finish. 'I'll ask some of the other girls to pick up a room or two extra if they can,' she said, and I nodded gratefully.

I took the service elevator to the top deck and stepped out into a corridor behind the kitchens, where the noise level would be shocking to anyone not used to it. 'Any complaints?' I asked loudly, and one of the servers passing through the kitchen made her way to me.

She leaned close and still had to speak loudly. 'A guy on twenty. He's still there. He claimed the drinks were watered down, so I comped him the cost.'

I nodded understanding and the girl grabbed a heavy tray and left. When no one else approached me, I turned and headed out to the table, putting on my best Guest Services smile.

The man in question was a crotchety old guy who'd already crossed my radar twice in the two days we'd been at sea. I sighed inwardly, but my tone was nothing but courteous when I approached his table. 'Hey, Rick, I heard you had a problem again today.'

'If you're going to charge me $10 for this fruity shit, it better not be watered-down fruity shit,' he growled, but he wasn't angry any more and the rant didn't have bite.

'Mind if I take a seat?' He gestured to the empty chair and I sat across from him and joined him in staring out over the turquoise water. 'You seem to be having a rough trip so far. Is there anything I can do?'

'You can tell your damned serving girls to stop trying

to cheat me,' he said. The first day, he'd called the help desk to complain that he thought a maid had rummaged through his luggage. Yesterday it had been a complaint that his breakfast coffee was too weak. I'd pulled up his guest information last night, expecting more of the same.

'I can do that, but I really don't think anyone *wants* you to have a bad time, here.' He said nothing, and I took a long pause before I spoke again, softly this time. 'I saw that you booked a double room.'

Rick let his head fall to his chest and scrubbed at his face with one broad hand, silent for a long moment. I waited. Sometimes Guest Services meant maid, complaint desk or escort. Sometimes it meant ship counsellor, sort of.

'We were going to celebrate our sixtieth anniversary,' he finally said, his voice rougher and softer than normal. I continued to wait in sympathetic silence. 'She died two months ago. Last thing she said to me was "Go on and enjoy the Caribbean for me." How can I enjoy it without her?'

'I don't know how to answer that, but I'm here to help. We have a single occupancy room available with a nice sea view if you would like to move. I can upgrade you for free, if that might help.' I'd gotten the offer pre-approved last night.

'I think maybe it would be nice not to see that empty bed,' he said quietly.

'If you enjoy shows, I can also get you our show

schedule. I'm sure it must be hard to laugh, but we have a great comedy show tonight. Would you like me to have our entertainment schedule delivered to your room?'

When he looked up, his eyes were shining, and I met them without flinching. 'Maybe I just needed someone to listen. Your schedule would be very nice. Thank you.'

'Do you remember where our service desk is?' He nodded. It was where he had placed the complaint about the maid. 'Head on up there and give them your name when you're ready. Let them know that Ally approved your room change. I'll call down and leave orders for your room and your entertainment information. You can move yourself, or we can get someone to help you shift your things, OK?'

He left me with a hug, and I sighed, feeling better about today. Maybe it wouldn't be such a rough trip for the poor old bastard after all.

'Well done.'

I spun around to find the source of the rich, deep voice. An athletically lean man stood behind me, smiling. His white teeth contrasted with the chocolate colour of his skin, and I had to do a quick mental check to be sure my tongue wasn't hanging out of my mouth at the sight of his open, short-sleeved button-down. With great effort I tore my eyes away from his defined abs and managed a 'Huh?'

'That guy was glaring at anyone who came within

ten feet of his table. In about five minutes you had him eating out of your hand.'

'Oh, yes, he was just having a rough time of it, and I helped smooth things over for him. Is there anything I can do for you?'

His wicked smile flashed again, and I felt myself grow warm as I read the message his hungry look implied. He traced his eyes slowly up and down my body before settling back on my face again. 'Not this second, I don't think,' he said. He tipped his drink towards me in salute and strode off, and I am not too proud to admit that I spent a few seconds admiring him from behind before I shook my attention back to the task at hand.

My usual trip around the deck to check on customer satisfaction was perfunctory today, and I was sneaking back below as soon as I had made sure there were no disasters I was missing. My thoughts kept returning to the gorgeous black man, and I wondered how I had managed to miss him before. A cruise ship can carry a population as large as some towns, but it's a relatively small town and you certainly tend to run into the same people over and over, even if they aren't making waves like poor old Rick.

I was still thinking of him as I grabbed the supply cart for a second time, checked the chart to find out what rooms still needed cleaning, and made my way to the sixth floor to get back to my secret second job. I had hours before I would be missed, so I plunged right in, letting my mind wander free as my body worked.

It wasn't long before my mind wandered to the stranger. His eyes had shone with interest and amusement, and I hadn't mistaken the approval he'd shown after undressing me with his gaze. It was against the rules to get involved with guests, but that didn't mean I couldn't fantasise about them. Especially the hot, muscled, just-my-type ones.

As I pulled up the sheets to make a bed, I finally couldn't resist any more. Even as I tucked the bedding into neat folds, my mind was envisaging a more adventurous use for the bed. I imagined finding out his name and room assignment and sneaking in and stripping down to my sexiest bra-and-panty set to wait for him. I'd be on the bed with the covers thrown back, my hair loose and flowing around my shoulders.

He would come in, maybe with a drink in his hand, and he would smile slowly as he took in the sight of me waiting for him. He'd take a slow sip and then set it down on a table as he approached me, and his kiss would taste like rum and pineapple. I imagined the way he would kiss down my neck, and I would turn my head and see the growing bulge tenting his shorts, and I would moan in wanton pleasure …

I squirmed, breathing hard and knowing better than to even try to do anything about my fierce arousal where a guest could catch me. I tried to concentrate on scrubbing, but my mind wouldn't leave it alone, and soon my imagination was back on his bed with him as he teasingly stroked my wet pussy through the lace of my panties, refusing to give me the satisfaction I craved.

In my imagination his hands drifted up higher, and he cupped my lace-clad breasts and found my nipples, rolling them in his fingers until they were so hard they could almost have sliced through the thin fabric. When he finally released the clasp of my bra to free them, I moaned, and the sound startled me out of my fantasy as I realised I'd actually moaned out loud.

I closed my eyes, panting hard, and tried to centre myself. Rooms. Cleaning. The damn toilets.

It made no difference. Within two more rooms I was breathing as heavily as ever as I imagined the way he would climb on top of me and fill me with his huge cock. I was so aroused that I could hardly see straight when I got to the last block of rooms I had to clean for the day.

In the second to last room, I found the magazines. The heavier top covers of the bed had been thrown back, and a small collection of magazines lay on the sheets. I reached for them to transfer them to the side table and froze with my arm extended when my mind registered the cover of the top magazine.

It showed a gorgeous naked blonde on her elbows and knees, her crossed arms barely keeping her nipples off display. Her eyes burned seductively, and behind her knelt a black man, his cock supposedly buried in her. The title of the magazine was *Mahogany Stud*. I bit back a whimper of arousal, checked the bathroom and even the closet to make sure the room was empty, and then hurried back to the bed.

I took a deep breath, flipped the magazine open and treated myself to page after page of incredibly sexy black studs impaling various women in a whole lot more detail than could be seen on the cover. I stopped at a particular page where a close-up caught a thick black cock poised at the opening of a glistening pussy, and it was all too easy for my already enflamed mind to imagine myself and my fantasy man as the subjects of the photo.

I reached down inside my slacks, staring at the photo and feeling that moment of anticipation myself as I slipped my hand into my panties and began to massage my excruciatingly swollen clit. I bit down on my lip, stifling my cries as I pictured him driving himself deep into me, and my body exploded in waves and waves of pleasure that left me weak in the knees and wavering on my feet.

Panting, satisfied and horrified that I'd just masturbated in a guest's room – with a guest's personal porn stash! – I practically ran to the bathroom to wash my hands and finish cleaning.

* * *

92

My boss showed some concern at our morning briefing the next day. 'You seemed really distracted last night when you were doing the rounds of the Palm Lounge. Everything OK?'

'I'm fine, it was just a long day. There, uh, there was a really sad old guy – you remember me mentioning the problems with Rick? – and I found out his wife just died. I did what I could, but I guess that sort of thing sticks with you.' I hadn't actually thought about Rick once since I'd called in his room change and left the upper deck, but I knew my boss would eat it up.

'Poor guy. I saw you upgraded his room? Hope he can enjoy his trip.' I sighed as the focus turned to other things. The truth was I'd been unable to concentrate the entire evening. It had been a mercy to get back to my own room and *really* release that sexual tension. I'd touched and teased myself until my skin tingled and it felt like the force of my arousal should be seeping from my pores, and then I'd brought myself over the brink with my favourite fat dildo, fucking myself way past the point of orgasm.

I had today off once the briefing was over, and I planned to finish the maid work as fast as I could and get back to my room for a repeat performance.

I dressed myself in a spare maid uniform since I would not have to spend my day running up and down the decks doing double duty. We'd arrived in Cozumel shortly after my morning meeting was concluded, so I knew most of the rooms would be empty as guests enjoyed their shore excursions. Still, it was good to present the proper image, just in case.

I hurried through the cleaning, keeping my mind firmly upon the task at hand, and very carefully made sure that the room with the magazines would be the last one of the day. I knew just being there would be enough to remind me, even if he'd put his stash away, and I wanted those thoughts fresh in my mind when I went off duty, not distracting me while I tried to work.

I was bone-tired by the time I got to that particular hall, but my heart still sped up when I spied the door. I carefully cleaned every other room on the corridor, skipping The Room until everything else had been finished. Finally, only that room stood between me and an afternoon of carnal pleasure.

I gave a quick knock, announced myself and used my universal key to unlock the door. The room had the same lived-in look as most of the other rooms, the bed unmade and clothes thrown over a chair, but I noticed sadly that the porn did not seem to be out, today. Not that it should be, I reminded myself.

The rumpled bed was first on the list of tasks to tackle, so I crossed the room and had just grasped the sheet when I heard the rattle of the bathroom door behind me. I spun, an apology ready on my lips, but it froze there when I saw who emerged from the head.

It was him. Of *course*, it was him. He was entirely shirt-less this time, and the dark of his nipples drew my eyes to his perfectly formed pecs before I could stop myself.

'Do you drive the ship, too?' he asked.

I blushed. 'Of course not. I'm not really a maid, either.' His eyes travelled the uniform, making the knee-length skirt feel like a mini with his appraising stare. 'I'm doing a favour for a friend.'

'Too bad, because I like the French maid bit even more than I liked that sexy pants suit,' he told me, and that spectacular white smile lit up his face again.

'I should, um, I should probably go. I'll send someone later, if you like. Sorry to disturb you.' My face was annoyingly flushed and my mind just kept replaying all of yesterday's fantasies for me.

'You cleaned in here yesterday, too,' he said. I started to deny it, but he added, 'I was just coming up the hall when you left with the cart. I hadn't meant to leave those magazines out for the maid to see, but I'm kind of glad it was you.' He stepped closer, narrowing the distance with each word. 'Did my collection … disturb you?' I faced him from inches away. It was too close and I couldn't breathe. I went to take a step back and fell over the bed. My pussy throbbed as I pictured him moving to place himself on top of me, and my breath came in short, aroused gasps.

The object of my desire stepped back, looking

apologetic. 'I didn't mean to scare you, miss. I'm sorry. You can leave, it's OK.' He started to step to one side, hands raised, but I shook my head and he paused, head tilted enquiringly.

'I'm not scared,' I whispered. My voice came out husky and thick with arousal, and I spread my legs a little, just enough to draw his attention to the movement. His dark eyes followed the motion and widened in understanding, and his smile spread slowly across his face as he got the message, loud and clear.

'Well then,' he said quietly, 'you didn't answer my question. What did you think of my ... reading material?'

'Not bad,' I managed to say. I took a shuddering breath and took the leap. 'How does it compare to the real thing?'

He laughed. 'Now *this* is room service.' He grabbed the bulge in his shorts and raised his eyes to me in challenge. 'Why don't you come here and find out?'

I stood slowly, not because I was unsure but because my legs were shaking. I'd never done something this crazy in my entire life, but the way he stood there stroking himself idly through his shorts set my entire body on fire, and I knew I couldn't turn away. He smiled as I stepped towards him, and continued to grin that challenge down at me from his superior height until I dropped to my knees in front of him. It took only a second to unbutton his shorts and pull them and his boxers down to his ankles.

His cock was only half hard and it was still easily the largest I'd seen, at least in person. I hummed a sound of approval and moved in close to burrow into the thick, musky black curls at the base. After taking his scent deep into my lungs, I moved back slightly and looked up at him. He smiled as he reached down to grab his cock and struck me gently across the face with the thick meat of it, beating it lightly against first one cheek and then the other.

He grew even thicker before my eyes, his pulse driving blood into his organ as he watched my upturned face. I sighed as I brought the tip close to my lips, breathing across it before I let my tongue snake out to taste him. His breath came in a rough hiss as my tongue traced the purple ridge of his crown, teasing him and drawing out the moment for myself.

My pussy pulsed in answer as he stroked his length a couple of times, and when he nudged the tip towards my lips again I opened up, taking as much as I could of him in my mouth and throat. I sucked and licked, swirling my tongue around his head before I pulled back and licked down the length of him and back again, and soon he was moaning and his hips were thrusting towards me. I purred as he grabbed at my hair, clumsily freeing it from my ponytail so that he could twist his fingers through it.

'So how do I compare?' he asked.

'Better than I'd hoped,' I said, grinning up at him. He stroked his hard length as he stared down at me, and I took the opportunity to study his cock. It was enormous, thick and long like something you would see in a porno, and my pussy clenched eagerly to think how well it would fill me. 'I could lose my job for this,' I said.

'But?'

'But I've been thinking of how much I wanted to fuck you since I met you on deck yesterday,' I said. My fingers drifted upwards and I started to unbutton the front of my maid's uniform.

'What a coincidence,' he joked. Then he added, 'I won't tell if you won't.' He reached down and grabbed my arms to bring me to my feet and pushed me gently back, guiding me towards the bed. By the time he thrust me back onto it, my top was unbuttoned to the waist. He followed me onto the bed, crawling up my body to my breasts where he pushed the fabric of my top out of the way and took my lace-covered globes in his hands. He licked and sucked at one nipple through the lace and then the other one, teasing me with the exotic sensations.

As I moaned and arched into his mouth, he let one hand drift down my body and past the skirt of my uniform, then up my leg towards the molten heat of my cunt. I gasped when he found my soaked panties, and lifted my hips to help him peel them off. He tossed them aside with a grin and returned to my centre, dipping his fingers into the wetness he found there.

'You sure weren't lying about wanting this,' he teased.

He smeared my cream down one side of my neck and then moved to lick it all away. His tongue left a trail of fire across my skin and chased shivers down my spine.

'I want you to stick that enormous cock in me,' I panted, 'and I want you to fuck me until I scream.'

He moaned hungrily in response and moved away from me, stopping between my legs to shove the skirt up over my thighs and bury his face in my pussy. I cried out in pleasure as his tongue found my clit and flicked over it, driving me closer to the edge. 'You sure you're ready for this?' he asked, and then he returned his attention to my pussy, licking and sucking as he thrust several fingers inside me and began to stroke.

'Yes!' I yelled, and then the pleasure grew almost unbearable in intensity and broke over me like a wave. 'Yes! God, yes!' I shouted, not caring who might hear. I moaned in incoherent pleasure for another minute before I could pant out the words, 'Fuck me. Fuck me now!'

He pulled a condom from the bedside table, rolled it over his huge erection and positioned himself between my legs. 'Is this what you want?'

'Yes! Oh, please, yes!' I didn't have to ask again.

He slid forward slowly at first, stretching my cunt wide – wider than I had ever experienced before, even with the toys I had considered adventurous. It was so intense it was almost painful as he forced my body to new dimensions, filling me like I'd never been filled before. I moaned loudly, loving the way he stretched me as he inched forward, then reared back just a little before forging ahead again. By the time he was seated fully inside me I was nearly crying with the intensity of the pleasure.

I had never experienced anything so incredible – I could feel him entirely inside me, stretching my pussy and filling every inch of me. He gave me a while to get used to the intensity of the sensation before he pulled back and plunged his entire length into me. I screamed as I came, this time. Distantly I was aware of him steadily screwing me into the bed, but all I could concentrate on were the lights bursting behind my eyelids and the jolts of pleasure that shot through me like electricity each time he buried his length in me.

When the sensations had faded somewhat, I opened my eyes to see his intense face over me. Then he moaned, and I watched as his face contorted in pleasure. My cunt tingled in sympathetic ecstasy and I squeezed around him, milking his orgasm.

He lay down across me, supporting just enough of his weight to keep from crushing me. 'I'm Michael,' he said into the pillow.

'I'm Ally.' An aftershock shuddered through my body. 'I live on a ship. I don't do relationships.'

'I'm on vacation alone because I'm too busy to bother with a girlfriend,' he countered.

'Cruise lasts three more days,' I said, smiling.

'Give me ten minutes and we can do that again, slower,' he said. 'What time you getting off tomorrow?'

Polar Bear Passion
Heather Towne

It was hot and humid and stuffy inside our small apartment. Chance banging me from behind only added to the heat.

I gripped the bedspread and gritted my teeth as I was rocked back and forth on my hands and knees by the big lug's impassioned pronging. His thick fingers dug into my waist, his muscular thighs slamming against my bum cheeks, his long, hard cock ramming deep into my pussy. Sweat dewed my face and body, my tits flapped, my blood boiled.

But just before we both skidded down the slippery slope of certain ecstasy, blasted past the point of no return, Chance suddenly pulled his plugging cock out of my steaming pussy and spun me over onto my back. He quickly swung his big body around, so that his knees were straddling my head, his gleaming cock hanging down over my flushed face.

I exulted at the change in position, more than happy to play along. I grabbed onto one of Chance's humped buttocks with one hand and grasped his hard cock with the other. He grunted, gushing hot, humid air all over my pussy. His head was bent down in between my legs, his strong hands gripping my trembling thighs. I licked the tip of his straining dick, just as he licked my brimming slit.

We both groaned. After two years of intense love-making and uninhibited experimentation, our sexual movements were coordinated for maximum pleasure. Chance dragged his wide, wet tongue through my blonde fur and over my engorged pussy lips, stroking me full of delight. I popped his bloated hood into my mouth and then sucked the swollen shaft inside.

I moaned around his dong, sending tremors of pleasure through his body like he was sending through mine, as he slurped hungrily at my slit. Half of his huge cock throbbed inside my mouth, my lips sealed tight around the veiny meat. I tasted my own pussy juices on his prick. Then I tasted more of Chance, deep and delicious, bobbing my head up off the bed, sucking on his cock in rhythm with him lapping my pussy.

It was sensationally erotic. If I hadn't been laid out flat on my back with the big guy pinning me down with his hands and tongue, I might well have fainted from the wicked licking Chance was giving my sex.

As it was, my face and body burned, and my bobbing head went dizzy. I grabbed onto both of Chance's big butt cheeks and dug my fingernails into the thick, mounded flesh, hanging on, sucking hard and high on his beefy cock.

We rapidly hurtled towards the getting off – and getting off hard – point again, our sucking and slurping stoking our fire to inferno. That's when Chance shifted again, back to the previous exciting position, so he could hammer us headlong into all-out joy.

He swung back around and rolled me over, pulled me up onto all fours, plunged his cock back into my pussy from behind. He grunted, I moaned, his cock filling my shimmering wetness, plugging me full of good feeling. He gripped my hips and pumped his, pounding into me at full ramming speed. Driving us through the last sexual barrier before total release.

Chance grunted and bucked in behind me. His cock sprayed, torching my burning tunnel. I tore a hand off the bedspread, thrust it down onto my pussy and rubbed my swollen clit, quickly joining my beau in blissful, blazing orgasm. I cried out my joy, coming and coming and coming.

As we snuggled in each other's arms afterwards, basking in the hot, sticky glow of our lust, Chance rumbled, 'So, babe, given any thought as to where you want to spend Thanksgiving?'

I grabbed my favourite plush polar bear from the collection of stuffed animals lining the headboard and kissed its button-black nose. 'No ... not really.'

When you live in a sub-tropical place like Florida, where are you supposed to go for a late-fall/early-winter break? The temperature was 90 degrees with 80 per cent humidity, after all.

I had Po kiss Chance on the mouth, then lumbered the furry white bear down the guy's broad chest and ribbed stomach to his cock, and got Po to bat the semi-shrunken appendage around with his big black paws. 'Maybe my parents in Texas?' I suggested.

Chance groaned. He grabbed onto Po's head at his lower head and shook the both of them. 'No way. I'm still getting over last Christmas.'

I flushed even hotter. It was getting uncomfortable, like it always did whenever the subject of my parents came up. I plopped Po down in between my breasts and stared thoughtfully into his glassy eyes.

And then I had a brainwave to escape the perpetual heatwave.

'How about Churchill? In Manitoba, Canada?'

Chance looked at me looking eagerly at him, at Po's nodding head. 'Say where?'

I scrambled up onto my knees. 'Yeah! I just saw a documentary on the place. I got a DVD when I made a donation to the World Wildlife Fund. It's way up north, located right on the migration route of polar bears. They come down from the Arctic in the winter to feed.'

Chance rolled his eyes.

'There're northern lights ... and a fort ... and it's the polar-bear capital of the world! It's really cool this time of year.' Po and I stared at the big guy with our most pleading expressions.

* * *

It wasn't cool. It was COLD! Minus 30 degrees Celsius when we stepped off the plane and ran for the tiny terminal. The windchill iced the temperature further down into the minus 40s. Typical late-November weather, our pilot informed us.

After packing everything warm we could lay our hands on, we'd flown out of steamy Florida up to chilly, snow-bound Winnipeg. Then we'd hopped aboard a smaller jet for the 1,000-kilometre trip north to Churchill.

'Cold enough for you now?' Chance chided me through chattering teeth, as we bundled into the van that drove us from the airport to our hotel.

And then the big brown-haired, blue-eyed hunk got even more sarcastic, when he made the shocking discovery that our hotel room didn't have a TV. 'Rustic, huh?' he snarked.

It was! There were wood beams in the ceiling, Inuit paintings on the log walls, soapstone carvings on the rugged, handcrafted furniture, and a ptarmigan feather on our pillows. 'Yes!' I exulted, hugging Po to my breast and breathing deep of the fresh, clean, crisp air.

The town had looked small from the air, and it wasn't much bigger on the ground. There were a few stores selling furs and native artwork and handicrafts, a number of hotels and restaurants catering to the eco-tourist trade, a recreation centre, a train station and a port facility on the frozen Churchill River that was apparently open only two months of the year.

Chance and I spent our first day exploring. The temperature had 'warmed up' to a bracing minus 20, so we could see each other's watering eyes and dripping noses under all the hoods and scarves. Hudson Bay was a vast frozen expanse of ice and snow, boulders piled up along what we believed was the shore, a rusted shipwreck stranded further out. The boat wasn't the *Discovery* that Henry Hudson himself had captained back in 1611. But we could certainly understand why a crew of Englishmen might get a little mutinous when forced to spend a winter on the shore of the huge ice-bound bay.

We took a snowmobile ride across the Churchill River to historic Prince of Wales Fort, roamed around there awhile. The fort had been built by the Hudson's Bay Company in 1717 to protect their fur trade from the French. The glare of the bright yellow sun shining off the dazzling white snow justified my packing our sunglasses.

By the time we got back to the hotel that night, we were starving. I'm not a big meat-eater, normally, but that 16-ounce elk steak really hit the spot.

At midnight, we assembled with ten other hardy tourists and were whisked out onto the tundra by all-terrain vehicle to watch the Northern Lights, or *aurora borealis*. The black sky was spectacularly lit up with flashes of green and pink and blue and purple, the stunning lights dancing in the heavens just above us. Even Chance had to admit it was better than any laser show.

Each couple was set up with a pup tent and a propane heater and a basket of locally produced food. We sat at the mouth of our tent and stared up at the Northern Lights in awe, noshing on cranberry jam and pemmican, moose jerky, smoked Arctic char and caviar (sturgeon eggs), sipping ice wine.

'Not bad, huh?' I commented, hugging Chance's arm around my shoulders and gazing up at nature's lightshow. Our breath came in white puffs, but the hissing heater kept us warm and toasty from behind.

'It's OK,' Chance acknowledged. Then the guy really got in touch with *his* nature, snaking his hand down my side and around onto my boob, squeezing me through my layers and layers of clothing.

'Mmm,' I murmured, his big, warm mitt making my breast shimmer. 'I'm starting to feel the heat again.'

We faced each other and rubbed noses. Then we

kissed, with our lips, Chance using both hands to maul my boobs.

The other tents containing the other tourists were scattered around us in a semi-circle, the closest ones about twenty feet away on either side. Everybody was gazing up at the flashing sky, spellbound – except for our three escorts who were standing sentry duty with their rifles. They were looking away from us, scanning the illuminated tundra for rogue polar bears.

Chance pushed me back, down onto the ground, inside the tent. He tried to climb on top of me, the lusty marauder. But I quickly squirmed around the other way so that my head was sticking out of the tent opening and I was still staring up at the sky. Making love by starlight was one thing; making love by the Northern Lights was something really special.

Chance covered my hot body with his. I grabbed his toqued head and kissed him, darted my tongue into his open mouth. We excitedly frenched, thrashing our tongues together, the heat rising externally and internally.

Chance fumbled with the zipper on my parka, my fleece hoodie, the buttons on my sweaters. He roughly yanked up my T-shirts and undershirt and finally my bra. I moaned around his tongue as he grasped my bare, buzzing breasts. Then I squealed with delight, when he bent his shaggy head down and slapped my tingling nipples around with his tongue.

'Yes, baby!' I gasped, the guy's warm, wet, swirling tongue making my nipples seize up with pleasure.

He suddenly inhaled half of one breast, pulling hungrily on it, vaccing hard. I arched my chest up into his hands and mouth, urging him on. He moved his head over to my other boob, shot up that surged nipple with his squeezing hand and urgently and heavily sucked on it. I saw even more stars and lights.

Chance gorged himself on my breasts. I was only too happy to feed his craving, thrusting my chest, my tits up into his clutching hands and chewing mouth. He shoved my boobs together and wagged his heavy tongue across both of my blossomed buds at once, staring up into my eyes.

I glared down into his, the shimmering Northern Lights and my seething passion reflected in the shining pair. Chance sucked up both of my nipples together, tugged on them with his thick lips. I rolled my head from side to side, overcome, overjoyed, as the manimal ravished my surging tits to my utter delight.

He released my boobs, mouth and hands. They simmered with remembered passion. Chance dropped his head down lower, licked my chest below the breasts, dragged his tongue down onto my rapidly rising and falling stomach. I grasped his bobbing head and buried my fingers in his hair. His tongue swarmed my bellybutton and swirled inside, and I arched up off the frozen ground with heated emotion.

110

His warm, moist tongue-tip writhed all around inside my sensitive bellybutton, swabbing me in sensation. And as he frenched my tummy, he dug a big paw into the layers and layers of my lower garments, and his roaming fingers found my juiced-up pussy. I gasped, shuddered, as Chance petted my pussy and tongued my bellybutton.

The Northern Lights were shut out by my squeezing eyelids, the electric energy show exploding inside me now. I spasmed repeatedly, my breasts and body jumping, Chance's twisting tongue and rubbing hand charging me up, generating pure, white-hot pleasure.

We had to share in the incredible night, erotically. It wasn't fair that I got all the razzle-dazzle. So I popped my eyes open and pulled Chance's head up. His tongue corkscrewed out of my stomach and his hand brushed over my slit. And then he was back on top of me, hotter and hornier than ever.

We kissed, frenched again, our tongues dancing together like the lights up above. Chance slid two of his fingers into my open mouth and I sucked on them, tasting the juices he'd swirled out of my pussy.

But there was just no way we could get out of all our cold-weather duds and free all of our charged-up naughty parts. Not in that confined space without attracting unwanted attention. So we got raw as we could outside in the great white north. Chance humped his hard cock against my wet pussy through four or five layers of clothing.

It felt wonderful – protected sex, Arctic-style. I wrapped my arms around Chance's neck and passionately kissed him, the iron-hard outline of his erection pumping up and down my wet, wildly tingling slit. Cold air swirled in from outside, hot air billowed out from inside, the dark skies were alive with brilliant, streaking colours.

We almost melted right through the permafrost. Then Chance grunted and spasmed on top of me, spurting into his longjohns. I moaned and quivered beneath the big guy, a wicked orgasm arcing all through me, thoroughly wetting my panties and sweatpants.

When we opened our eyes again and rolled them upwards, there was a round moonface partially blotting out the Northern Lights. 'Please, you have any more caviar?' the man asked, a wide grin splitting his beaming face. 'Power-ful aphrodisiac, yes?'

* * *

The next day, we ventured back out onto the tundra to see the polar bears. I was almost as excited as the night before in the tent, at the prospect of viewing the giant white bears up close – though there was no guarantee we'd actually see any.

'I've got a surprise for you,' Chance said, the smile freezing on his handsome mug as we hurried from our hotel to the tundra buggy depot on the edge of town.

'Tundra buggies' were really old school-bus bodies mounted on giant, tractor-sized tyres, pulled by a huge diesel cab. Most of the seats were removed inside to allow people to move around, the floor lowered, and a guard-railed viewing platform added to the back, outside. The vehicles were so high off the ground that a bear couldn't rear up on its hind legs and snatch a tourist out of an open window.

We walked past a number of the white-painted buggies, and then turned a corner. And there was Chance's surprise – a fully pimped-out tundra buggy for our private amusement and enjoyment.

The body and cab were painted metallic black, like a limousine, the windows darkly tinted; there were giant silver hubcaps on the huge wheels and a 'party' deck out the back complete with a hot tub. Silver letters spelled out 'Snuggy Buggy' on the side.

The chauffeur-attired driver tipped his cap and helped us climb up the steel stairs of the vehicle. The interior was warm, well-appointed, black-leather comfort, complete with a bar, strobe ball and sound system.

'Wow!' I marvelled. 'How much did it cost to rent this thing?'

Chance smiled, hugged me tight and squeezed my bum. 'Nothing is too good for my bare baby.'

A tear sprang to my eye – and my pussy.

The driver started up the engine with a roar, and we

lurched forward. Chance and I were all by ourselves in the back, ensconced in luxurious privacy.

As the big guy mixed a couple of drinks, I slid open a window and stuck my head outside. We were lumbering across the tundra headed northwest. Unbroken, sun-blasted white stretched out before us.

We drank, got naked. It was hot in the Snuggy Buggy; we made it scorching.

As Chance hung his head out the open window to keep an eye out for polar bears, I went down on my knees on the wall-to-wall carpet, eye to eye with Chance's third eye. I gripped his erection and pumped it, slapped the mushroomed hood with my tongue. He bucked, almost bumping me right through the side of the giant all-terrain vehicle.

He looked down at me wedged in between his legs and the metal wall. I pointed up at the window with my free hand, and he reluctantly went back to bear-watching duties. I cupped his hairy balls with that hand, squeezed the heavy pair. I pumped shaft with my other hand, sucked knob with my mouth.

I sealed Chance's cap tight between my lips and wet-vacced the bulbous cocktip. He groaned and quivered. I tasted pre-come, hot and salty, as I sucked his hood, stroked his shaft, twisted his balls. It all tasted so good I had to have more, so I pushed my head forward, opening my mouth up as wide as it would go. Half of Chance's

enormous dong filled my face, ballooning my cheeks and bumping up against the back of my throat.

Chance rattled the side of the buggy, his muscular legs shaking. I kept him locked up tight, pulsating in my moist, satiny mouth for a moment, still working his shaft and balls with my hands. Then I pulled my head back and pushed it forward, glided my mouth up and down Chance's cock, blowing the big boy.

'That's it, baby!'

I popped his prick out of my mouth in a spray of saliva. 'You see something out there?' I gasped.

He looked down at me. 'No! No! Don't stop. I'll keep a lookout.'

I grinned up at him, swirling my tongue all around his shining knob. Then I inhaled half of his pipe all over again, resumed sucking, tight and wet and fast.

His balls seized up in my clutching hand. I had to taste them, too, before it was too late. We were out in the wilds, after all, the perfect place to release my inner animal. And what better place for some hot teabagging than the frozen northlands?

I slid my tongue and lips off Chance's cock and dipped my head lower, swatted the man's sac with my outstretched tongue. He grunted and spasmed.

I juggled his hairy pair around on the end of my tongue, breathing deep of my guy's intimate musky manliness. Then I sucked his sac right into my mouth, swallowing it whole.

'Fuck!' he hollered, his cock batting my forehead and nose.

I sucked on his balls, billowing my cheeks, really turning up the heated pressure on his sperm bag.

'I-I ... think ...'

Not already, I thought, regretting my erogenous mouth-milking now. I wanted the big guy shooting off into my pussy, not into the air.

'I see something!' Chance gulped.

I spat out his nuts and sprang to my feet, shoved him back, spun around, shot my head out the window. And I spotted a tiny black dot way off in the crystal-clear distance.

'Polar bears coming up,' the driver crackled over the intercom, making me almost jump out of my skin.

As we trundled forward, closer, I saw that the black dot I'd spotted was actually the wet black nose of a mama polar bear, rearing her head to sniff at the air and look at us. Two adorable snow-white cubs quickly scampered into view as well.

I just about wet myself with excitement. Cold air flowed over my bare tits and chest, cooling my fervour not a bit, making my nipples swell hard and tingly. Then big, warm hands covered my breasts, rolled my rigid buds. I barely felt Chance's paws on my breasts as he groped from behind, his hard cock thrusting against my bum. The mama bear lumbered closer, raising and lowering its huge head, the baby bears following behind.

The Snuggy Buggy jerked to a stop about a hundred yards away from the bear family, and the driver shut off the engine. Silence enveloped the winter wonderland, until I squealed, 'Look, they're coming towards us!'

Chance's hands were down on my bum cheeks, spreading them, his hot, wet tongue surging in between my legs and slurping at my pussy. I shuddered, staring at the approaching polar bears. They were only twenty feet away, curious about the huge vehicle and the naked, tanned blonde woman hanging out the window.

Chance plunged two thick fingers into my juiced-up slit and pumped, sinking his teeth into my buttocks. I giggled with glee. The baby bears were cavorting with each other behind their mama. She was almost right below us now, sniffing at one of the buggy tyres. Her shaggy coat was white and yellow, her eyes and nose coal-black, paws huge with long, sharp, black claws. Clouds of steam billowed out of her nostrils as she snuffled.

Chance stood up and crowded in behind me again, his pulsating erection sliding in between my butt cheeks and pumping. He grasped my tits again, rolled my nipples, kissing and licking and biting into my neck. I quivered with delight, watching the two smaller bears jump on one another and wrestle around, while big mama wandered around to the other side of the buggy.

'Quite a show, huh?' Chance breathed in my ear, frotting my bum cleavage.

I exhaled. 'Yeesss!'

He stuck the bulbed tip of his cock into my pussy and thrust home. His thick shaft filled me with even more pleasure, and I gasped. The baby bears looked up at me with their big eyes, their black button noses twitching.

Chance churned his cock back and forth in my pussy, groping my tits, nuzzling my neck. Cold front and hot back met up and suffused me in shimmering warmth, as Chance pumped faster and faster.

I dropped my head and moaned, gripping the edge of the window. And when I popped my eyes open again, I was looking directly into the huge, wet eyes of mama bear. She'd reappeared and risen up against the side of the vehicle. She rocked the buggy one way, Chance and me the other, her and my mouth hanging open.

'Fuck, yeah!' Chance snarled, pounding into me. Then he bucked, bellowed, blasted hot spurts of semen into my melting core. He crushed my tits in his hands, slamming against my butt, ramming and creaming my pussy.

Mama lifted her head high and let out a roar, showing off her big, sharp, yellow teeth and giving me a heated blast of seal-breath. I joined her call of the wild, rearing up on my toes and wailing my joy, orgasm searing up from my cock- and come-filled pussy and blazing through my bare body.

I tried to lunge down and fling my arms around the majestic arctic bear, overcome with emotion. Chance had to frantically pull me back into the buggy. Polar bears look beautiful, yes, but make no mistake, they're man-eaters. And so was I, when I intimately thanked Chance again for *coming*along with me on the marvellous northern vacation – back in the safe, cosy confines of our hotel room.

Welcome to Spain
Chrissie Bentley

I could see the battered old red bus coming from the top of the hill, rounding the last bend in the road before it turned into the cobbled marketplace. I paused for a moment, hoping that he'd actually caught it; even Peter's mother complained that his itinerary was vague, although he'd been adamant that this was his next halt, if only so he could pick up the money he'd called to ask her to wire, and hang out at the festival that was taking place that day.

He was true to his word. The mid-morning crowds were already surging back and forth across the marketplace, but I recognised him the moment he stepped off the bus and into the moist heat that had long since reduced my silk dress to translucence. Looking around at the village as he adjusted his hat, he reminded me of the shady sidekick in some old black-and-white Humphrey

Bogart movie, up to no good in a small foreign town that itself could barely have changed in fifty years. I'd been here a day and, if it wasn't for the satellite dishes on a handful of rooftops, and the cellphone tower that towered over the church, I'd swear they turned back time at the city limits.

I started to move towards him, pushing through the revellers as they swayed to the first of the day's musical attractions. Peter hadn't seen me. In fact, even if he did happen to look in my direction, I doubted he'd spot me with the sun in his eyes. A little ahead of me, however, a couple of teenagers did see me, and glanced up and whistled loudly. 'Hey, Senorita!' The state of my dress with the sun at my back – they could probably see right through it. Slightly self-consciously (wishing I was wearing more than a thong!), I smiled back at them but I kept moving, dodging around a vast woman armed with a massive basket of onions, and came to halt a few paces in front of Peter.

'So you made it, then?'

He stopped and squinted comically. I could see his mind trying to make sense of the picture before him. The last time he saw me, we were back in the States, the week before he left for a summer hiking trip around southern Europe.

'Chrissie?'

I enjoyed his confusion. 'I said, you made it, then.'

He nodded, his face still a mask of bafflement. 'But what are you –'

'I fancied a break,' I said with a smile. There was no point getting into explanations. They were boring and, besides, I would be back in Madrid on Monday, for the chain of business meetings that winkled me out of New York City in the first place. This was just a weekend diversion and, like I told his mother, Peter was the only guy I knew in Spain. So of course I had to look him up.

I walked alongside him as we manoeuvred through the crowds, waited while he picked up his money from the little Western Union office, and resisted the temptation to step in to help when it became clear he had only a basic grasp of the language. Somebody obviously didn't pay attention to Spanish classes at High School. But he sorted it out in the end and, as we stepped back into the sunlight, I locked his arm in mine. 'Have you booked a room any place?'

He shook his head. 'I thought I'd find something once I got here.'

'Good luck.' The festival drew revellers from miles around, and most of them stayed through the night. I doubted whether there was a room to be had any place in town. 'But never mind. You can crash at mine.'

Again he treated me to a look of bemusement, but I just laughed and pulled him along. We strung our way through the crowds, doubling down narrow alleyways to avoid the thickest crushes, circling through the maze of winding back streets that, thankfully, I'd already committed to memory when I negotiated them on my way to meet him. Finally, as the stalls and sideshows began to thin, we reached the blue-tiled walls of the hotel, slipped in through a door that you'd never have noticed if you hadn't known it was there, and crossed the ornately landscaped courtyard.

He whistled. 'You don't do these things cheaply.'

'No,' I agreed. 'But why would I want to?'

The uniformed concierge handed me my key. He looked, I must admit, a little askance at my unannounced guest, but I'd iron that out later. Then we boarded the rattletrap elevator that had definitely seen better days, and finally fell into my room, grateful for the sudden breath of cool air that broke the heat of the un-air-conditioned hallways.

I lit an incense burner on the mantel, squirted some patchouli into the air and gestured towards the open window. 'There's stables directly underneath us, and the smell can get a little ripe in the heat,' I explained, with the recently acquired air of a seasoned traveller. 'This takes the edge off it.'

Peter laughed. 'Don't bother explaining. It's a lot more exotic if you don't.' Then, 'But speaking of exotic, do you mind if I take a quick shower? After that bus ride, I'm feeling a little fragrant myself.'

'Go ahead.' I watched him as he went into the bathroom, waited till I heard the hiss of the water and the accompanying gurgle of ancient pipes, then stripped off my dress and hung it by the window to air out a little. Still sweating in my bikini, I curled up on the bed, watching the lizard I'd seen on the ceiling this morning. He (or she) crouched motionless in the corner by the window, or at least that's the impression he wanted to give. But every few moments a lengthy tongue would dart out and snatch something out of the air, and an unwary insect would wind up his lunch. Good pickings! Unbidden, a curious thought crossed my mind. I wonder if lizards enjoy oral sex? With tongues like that, they ought to.

I heard the clunk of the shower switching off. 'Towels in the airing cupboard,' I called through the closed door. There was an answering grunt and the sound of some rummaging, then the door opened. I shifted my shoulders and allowed my head to dangle over the edge of the mattress as Peter stepped out of the bathroom, a towel around his waist, while he vigorously dried his hair with another.

'I needed that,' he murmured through his motions. I grinned. 'I bet you did.' Then I stretched out both of my arms and clasped him by the knees. He stepped closer, and I tugged gently at the towel. It slipped down, but I kept my eyes trained firmly on his, trying to overlook just how comical he looked with his arms frozen in surprise above his head, his hair a wild tousle around the towel. People have said my eyes are my best point (people who've only seen me fully clothed, that is), and I won't disagree. Peter certainly seemed to be drinking them in, gazing back at me, his own face a wonderful confusion of bewilderment, surprise and anticipation.

It was time to break the spell. My hands were still on his knees; I pulled gently and he toppled forward, catching himself just in time to avoid falling on top of me, his legs parted behind my head and his cock just inches away. I grasped it in one hand, fat and soft and as unsuspecting as he seemed to be. Hah! Just how I like them to start with.

Mustering some grace and regaining his balance, he shuffled forward as his arms held his weight above the bed, then I pulled him to my lips and rolled the fleshy head of his still soft cock against lips that I'd just moistened with my tongue. There was a twitch as the blood began to rush in and I held him in my mouth as he hardened, sucking a little but mostly not moving, thrilling as his weight and thickness stretched my lips wider and pushed my tongue down.

I wondered why this had never happened before? How it was that I'd known Peter since college, and – with one completely out of character (yeah, Chrissie, keep telling yourself that) exception – we'd never gone further than a few drunken fumbles, and the half-spoken agreement that, sometime, we really ought to sleep together? Well, that sometime was now.

I remembered the night I met him, one of those nights where the music was so loud that you had to shout even when you whispering, and the moshpit was so crowded that you had no choice but to move with the rest of the audience, a rhythmic swaying and surging that threatened to topple you off balance, even as the people packed against you made certain that you wouldn't ever fall.

I closed my eyes and went with the flow, only dimly aware of all the points on my body where others were squashed against me – an elbow here, a shoulder there, a purse somewhere else – and I don't know what it was about that pressure on my ass but I knew it wasn't anything I'd have expected to find. I turned my head as much as I could and the guy standing behind me caught my eye and smiled, which was when I knew for sure what it was. He had a hard-on like you wouldn't believe and the only thing stopping it from sliding up my ass were his jeans and mine.

I tried to wriggle away but couldn't, the crowd was too thick. And part of me, I realised, wasn't trying too hard, either. There's something oddly arousing about having a complete stranger just a few millimetres of denim away from fucking you up the ass, and when a particularly hard surge separated us for a moment, I was shocked to find myself feeling disappointed. He was still behind me,

126

I knew, but his body had changed its angle just enough that the wonderful pressure I'd been riding for so long was gone. And I missed it.

I wriggled my ass, hoping to make contact again. Nothing. Just the hardness of his hips ... but at least I knew I was close. I shifted from one foot to the other, stepped a little to the left – ah, that's better. He was still off target but an inch or two more – and then I felt him again, hard between my butt cheeks, and I wondered what had changed to make him feel so much more 'real'? Which was when I reached behind me with one hand and came into contact with flesh. Hard, hot flesh.

I turned again, and he was still looking at me. Smiling, but not in a creepy, scary way. It was a challenge, and I shocked myself when I realised it was one I intended to rise to. The volume of the music, the heat of the crowd, the sudden unexpectedness of everything else, each one hit me like a hammer and I curled my fingers around his cock, moved away slightly to give myself room, and began gently jerking him off to the rhythm, long hard tugs that pulled the breath from his body, short, fast twists that just seemed to make him harder.

My wrist was twisted but I didn't care. I just kept on jerking him and when he came, a sudden flood that splashed hot on my fist, I kept going, massaging him back to softness as his hand touched mine to let me know I should stop. I wiped my hand dry on his jeans and turned my attention back to the concert, smiled as I felt him stuff something into my pocket – it turned out to be his phone number, scrawled on a torn cigarette box – and the next time I turned around, he was gone.

Now he was back.

The position in which I was lying made it difficult to move my head much. Holding him hard with my palms clamped to his butt, I began swaying his hips back and forth, to and fro, feeling him slipping in and out of my mouth. Occasionally I'd stop, hold him still while I sucked or, breaking for a much-needed breath, lapping my tongue around his shaft, across his balls. I drew one into my mouth, sucked it hard and then released it abruptly. He gasped aloud, and I felt him tense as I set to work on the other.

I raised my head and looked down my body. Peter hung over me, his eyes closed tight, his mouth wide open. I ran one hand along his torso as far as I could reach, tweaked a nipple and smiled as he gasped again. 'Just making sure you're awake down there.' I smiled, then pulled him back into my mouth.

'Oh, I'm awake all right.' I didn't need to coax him this time – his hips were moving of their own accord, driving his hot meat into my mouth, harder and faster as he realised that I wasn't going to stop him for anything. My fingers crept across his butt to his anus, stroked the sensitive opening slightly, before I allowed one fingertip to slip gently in and out, echoing his thrusts.

His breathing was hard, loud. I left his ass and gripped his balls, tense and tight – oh, but I desperately needed to catch my breath, too. I hung on for as long as I possibly could, breathing through my nose, but his thrusts were unending, his excitement still building. I had to pop him out of my mouth, just for a second ... jerking him hard as I drew a deep breath, and then hearing him cry out as he finally came, an unending jet of scalding white that spattered across my chest, pooled in my cleavage, even streaked my belly.

He rolled to one side and landed flat on his back, breathing heavily. 'Wow, welcome to Spain,' he whispered.

'Welcome, indeed.' I glanced towards the window, out at the reddening sky. It was already early evening – my God, how long did he keep it hard for? Why had we never slept together before? I was kicking myself!

I sat up and unclipped my bikini top. Amazingly, very little of his juice had actually hit it, but it would certainly get sticky if I didn't move it now. I slipped off my panties as well and, as Peter reached for me, I slid over to sit on his chest, enjoying the prickle of his hairs against my buttocks, and the slightest hint of his breath on my dampening pussy.

'That was wonderful,' he breathed.

'I know,' I shot back at him. 'I just wish I hadn't needed to breathe quite so soon.'

His brow wrinkled quizzically, and so very lovably. 'It's just as well that you did. I haven't come that hard in years.'

'Like I said,' I replied. 'I just wish I hadn't needed to breathe.' I leaned forward and kissed his forehead. 'Oh, don't try and work it out. I'll show you another time.'

With his eyes watching me like a hawk, I traced a finger through the stickiness in my cleavage, raised it to my lips and sucked the moisture away. I felt his hands on the small of my back, drawing me closer to his face. Ladling up another fingertip of the drying cream, I wiped it lightly against the lips of my pussy, just a split-second ahead of his tongue. I felt him draw back a little, but I laid one hand on the back of his head and pressed him forward again. The next lick was tentative, but delightful in its uncertainty, and I wanted to feel that again.

Two fingers this time, and a glob of white that I deliberately smeared around my clit. A fast learner. He went for it immediately, his tongue swirling around that taut little nub, the sensations instantly chasing away any other schemes that I might have had brewing. I threw my arms behind me, letting them take my weight, my head hanging back, my eyes closed tight. Outside, I could hear the carnival traders packing up as a fresh wave of street musicians arrived to take their place, playing for the tourists who would now be flocking to the restaurants and cafés, or gathering to dance in the market square.

I heard violins and guitars, and there a drum beat, one among many, but louder than the rest, deeper and more insistent. I caught it with my ears, harnessed it in my hips, and began slowly grinding its rhythm against Peter's face, thrilling as he picked up the same pattern with his tongue and ran with it, licking and flicking and sucking, face-fucking. Was that singing I could hear now? Or my own cries? I felt my orgasm gathering force within me, up from my legs, down from my belly, in from my ass, deep down inside of me, closer and louder and faster and there. Right NOW.

Now it was my turn to collapse in a heap, panting and gasping, and laughing as well, as Peter rolled with me and suddenly flipped around. His mouth was on mine now, his chest pressed against my breasts and, down below, a miraculous hardness that did not even need to knock. It just slid right in, filling me with a glorious warmth, an indescribable weight, an irresistible pressure.

My legs wrapped around his back and my arms reached up to meet them, gripped my feet and pulled them further apart. Peter was fucking me like a sewing machine, hard and fast, and not missing a single beat between strokes. Raising my head to bite his shoulder, I caught sight of us reflected in the mirror on the wardrobe at the foot of the bed. Ah, that's why they placed it so close, I smirked to myself. I wonder why I never thought of that before?

The room was darkening fast, but the dying light only added to the fascinating show. I could see his balls hanging down, doing their best to mask the shaft that plunged in and out, but I captured a glimpse of it anyway, as my hungry pussy lips sucked at the hard flesh, pulling him back inside.

You know how, sometimes, you'll be talking to someone, and they're bemoaning the fact that their sex life's so straightforward, that there's no adventure any more, no excitement left and no real passion? Believe me, it's there. You just have to see it from the right angle. The tongue on the clitoris, the lips around the knob-end, the cock crashing into the spread, red cunny, they're all present and correct. It's just that when you're in the midst of doing it, you usually have no way of seeing it. I could see it, and it was getting me even hotter than I already was.

I pushed my weight against Peter's body, held him tight in mid-gyration and, with more strength than I knew I possessed, forced him onto his back. He rolled willingly and only sighed when I disconnected our bodies for a moment, as I swivelled around on his hips, my back to his face, my ass on his belly, slipping him back inside of me as he ran his hands up my spine, and then reached around to caress my breasts.

I was facing the mirror now, and I began moving slowly. This angle can be tricky sometimes, it's all too easy for his cock to slip out ... there, it just did. I gently guided him back inside and lay my hand on my snatch, to hold him fast while I kneaded his balls, and let my palm flicker across my clit. It felt as hypnotic as it looked.

I wished we'd left a light on. It was growing darker by the minute, and the only illumination was whatever crept in with the music from the courtyard below. And then, whoa! Suddenly the entire room lit up as a massive set of floodlights clicked on in the gardens. Now it was as bright as day, and at last I could see every move we made, every plunge, every thrust, every single drop of juice that caught the light and glistened in my pubes and on his shaft, dripping and oozing, so wet, so wonderful. And I could feel myself coming again, as his thrusts grew more urgent and I knew that he was as well. I ground my hand against my clit, willing us both to make it together – and we did, although as my hand flew back to the mattress for support I felt, more than saw, his cock pop out again and shoot its payload hot across my thigh.

I almost spoke, a flippant 'damn, missed again' poised on my tongue. But the words were lost in my throat and, besides, who knew if he would even know what I was talking about? Instead I rolled over and kissed him hard on the mouth, and it was only after we'd lain there, not moving, for a while, that he finally spoke.

'You noticed the mirror as well, then?'

'Noticed it? I put it there,' I lied laughingly.

'I wondered. I've never watched myself before. It's like starring in your own porno movie, isn't it?'

'Except there's no director around to shout "cut" at the wrong moment,' I agreed. 'The only drawback is, you can only watch it the one time. There are never any reruns on the Looking Glass channel.'

He eyed me curiously for a moment. 'Would you want to watch something like that again?'

'So long as I owned the only copy.'

'I'd download it onto your laptop myself.' He stood, crossed the room to his luggage, and pulled out a carrying case that I knew, before he'd even opened it, contained a video camera. He pointed it at me and adopted an atrocious Hollywood accent. 'Lights ... action ... sound?'

I laughed. 'You're on. But remember, you're just the cameraman. And when I say "shoot" –' I paused and squeezed his balls '– I want to see you shoot.'

* * *

I awoke late, and was surprised to find Peter still curled up beside me. The bus out of town, the only bus of the day, left at 8, and we'd gone to sleep in the belief that he would be aboard it, and we'd catch up again when he returned to the United States. For a moment I thought he must have overslept but, as I sat up, he rolled over to face me.

'So, what do you have planned for today?'

I stroked his face. 'Couldn't tear yourself away, then?' It took me a moment to adjust to the silence outside, and then I remembered. When the bus went, most of the tourists went with it. The festival was over, and there was nothing else to keep them here.

'I thought about it, but hell. Europe will still be out there tomorrow. You, on the other hand, may not be. Not if you have to be in Madrid on Monday. So I figured I'd stay.'

I kissed him and snuggled down beneath the thin sheet that covered our naked bodies. In my mind I could still hear the drumming that had finally lulled us to sleep, around the same time as it awoke the dawn chorus. Out in the hallway, a radio was playing Al Stewart's 'Year Of The Cat', one of my all-time favourite songs, so mysterious, so sensual. Relaxing to a musical medley I couldn't resist, I took one of Peter's tiny nipples in my mouth and sucked gently at it before I began inching my way very slowly down his body.

Watching again one of the things that he'd filmed me doing last night had given me an idea ... something I wanted to try while it was still fresh in my mind. Plus, the hotel didn't offer room service, and I really needed to put something in my mouth.

Cruise Control
Elizabeth Coldwell

Madeira is beautiful as dawn breaks, the sun coming up over the tree-studded hills surrounding Funchal Bay, turning the clouds a pinkish-grey and bathing the sea with soft golden light. Songbirds wake and chirrup as the island slowly comes to life, welcoming the promise of another glorious day in paradise.

Allison saw nothing of this. As she had done every morning since the cruise began, she waited patiently in the cabin on B Deck, naked and in a classic display position with thighs spread wide, while Stuart jogged his regular half-dozen laps of the promenade deck. She might have been able to persuade him to give up his addiction to checking for work e-mails every few minutes – his phone lay on the cabinet beside their desk, switched off and forgotten for once – but even on holiday he still insisted on keeping up his regular fitness routine.

A nagging cramp had formed in Allison's left calf, and she longed to stretch out, easing the discomfort, but, convinced Stuart would somehow know she'd disobeyed his clear instructions by changing position in his absence, she remained where she was. Not long till he returned, she told herself; he was always back in the cabin well before the steward arrived, bringing their breakfast. Though even then she'd have to wait till Stuart had showered and dressed before she could eat. Rules were rules, after all.

Not that she should be complaining. How long had they talked about exploring Stuart's need to dominate, and hers to submit to him, in more depth? At home, they only played at being master and slave, setting aside time at weekends when she could willingly follow his instructions. The fantasy of living in those roles 24/7 fuelled their desires, made them dream of situations where it might be possible, but both knew it could only ever be a fantasy, constrained as they were by the demands of the real world, and the need to earn money and pay their bills on time.

But here, removed from everyday life and the people who knew them, those demands no longer applied. There was nothing to stop Stuart dominating her from the moment he woke, and she'd loved every last one of the deliciously kinky things he'd done to her.

The dress she'd be wearing for their excursion to Funchal later this morning already lay on the bed, picked out by Stuart before he left for his jog. A long, loose sundress in a red and white batik pattern, one of his favourites. She didn't know whether he'd selected any panties for her to wear, but she suspected not, knowing how much he loved having her bare and available beneath her respectable outer clothes. Her cuffs lay beside the dress: two wide leather bands inlaid with a delicate silver and turquoise pattern, giving them the look and feel of expensive jewellery. Only the two of them knew the secret of the cuffs' design; that the silver loops adorning them had been designed to link together, locking Allison's wrists in place behind her back till Stuart chose to release them. Anyone who'd seen them walking through the streets of Santiago de Compostela, following in the footsteps of centuries of pilgrims, or exploring Lisbon's old town, with its Moorish-influenced architecture and wrought-iron balconies festooned with trailing flowers, would have noticed how Stuart kept a solicitous hand in the small of his wife's back, guiding her passage as they walked, and smiled at the sight of his old-fashioned courtesy. They couldn't know he kept his hand there to disguise the locked cuffs, or that as he pointed to some historic sight or other and bent his head close to her ear, he was more than likely whispering, 'When we get back to the ship, I'll have you down on your knees, sucking my cock till I come in your mouth …'

If there hadn't been an excursion planned for today, he'd have expected her to spend the day naked while they were in the cabin, or sunbathing on their balcony. He allowed her to dress for dinner, but always in the skimpiest of outfits and with no underwear, so he was free to fondle her under the table as they ate. Even if they were invited to dine at the captain's table during the course of the cruise, as they surely would be, he'd make her sit there with her skirt hiked up and her thighs spread wide, him playing with her wet, needy pussy while she attempted to make polite conversation with her fellow dinner guests.

'Maybe I'll invite him to join in,' Stuart would murmur in her ear as they discussed this scenario in increasingly explicit detail. 'Let him finger your cunt, or slip a finger into your arsehole. You'd love that, wouldn't you?'

She couldn't deny the image excited her. They'd often talked about offering her to another man, letting him use her in ways that thrilled her just to think about. But she knew that, in reality, her husband would fight shy of introducing a third party into their games, with all the complications it might bring. Taking subtle control of her throughout the course of the holiday – from selecting her wardrobe to deciding what she'd eat for dinner, and whether she'd be allowed a glass of wine with her meal – had already been enough of a step into the unknown to satisfy both of them.

Thinking about dinner, and wine, made her stomach rumble. What might Stuart have selected for her breakfast this morning? Fruit compôte with yoghurt and a drizzle of honey, a flaky, buttery *pain au chocolat*, or scrambled eggs and a couple of rashers of crisply grilled bacon? She'd only know when the steward arrived, bearing their tray.

The option of steward service had been a big part of the reason Stuart had booked them into a suite – that, and the extra privacy it afforded them, with their own balcony where Allison could go naked without causing a commotion. Having a whirlpool bath in their en suite bathroom didn't hurt, either. She grinned to herself, thinking of how she and Stuart had fucked in that tub the night before, before he'd carried her to the bed, blindfolded her and taken her in the arse.

They'd had so much sex over the last few days; it had been like being on their honeymoon all over again. No, better than their honeymoon. Then, their sex life had been strictly vanilla, exciting enough in its way, but lacking the complexity their BDSM adventures provided. It had taken a while to learn what really turned them on, but once they had, they'd never looked back ...

The sound of a key card being slotted into the door brought Allison back to awareness of her surroundings. At last Stuart was back. She fought the urge to rise up and throw her arms around him, greeting him with a kiss; he expected her to wait as she was, eyes downcast, until he gave her the instruction to stand. Not even permitted to speak until she'd been spoken to, she bit back the cry of alarm that rose to her lips when she heard his voice.

Instead of his usual words of greeting, he was saying, 'That's it, if you'd just like to bring the tray in and set it down ...'

Despite her instructions, Allison couldn't help but look up, needing to know who Stuart was addressing, and why he'd allowed them to step inside the room when she was here, waiting for him with her thighs spread wide and her most intimate places on display.

It had to be one of the stewards. Though that might not be entirely bad news; one of the men who brought their breakfast, Ricardo, was rather gorgeous, with thick, wavy black hair and a wicked twinkle in his dark-chocolate eyes. She wouldn't mind him getting an eyeful of her cunt, trusting him to be discreet enough not to blab what he'd seen to his fellow crew members. But it wasn't Ricardo who stood alongside Stuart, or any of the other male stewards. Her husband's companion was a tall, whip-thin blonde dressed in the familiar white uniform with its fussy gold epaulettes, her eyes fixed on Allison with an expression that fused amusement with just a dash of contempt. She might never have met the woman before, but Allison recognised the dominant aura surrounding her.

The woman's kitten heels clicked across the cabin floor as she walked over to set down the breakfast tray.

'What's happening?' Allison wanted to ask. 'Why have you let her in here?' But until Stuart gave her permission she was compelled to remain mute, pleading for answers with her eyes.

At last, her husband broke the silence. 'You may get to your feet, slut.'

Allison wanted to protest even as she clambered upright, her cramped limbs protesting at finally being forced to move. It had taken her a little while to feel comfortable with Stuart using that word to describe her, and being called 'slut' in front of a woman she'd never even met before seemed even more humiliating. But wasn't that the point? she asked herself.

'This is Birgit,' Stuart continued. 'I happened to bump into her as she was coming down the corridor, and we've just been having a little chat. Great timing, eh?'

Allison said nothing, just watched as her husband peeled off his sweat-soaked T-shirt. The sun had tanned his skin to a light honey shade, and he looked good, with the taut stomach and well-toned biceps that paid testament to his exercise regime. Oblivious to their guest, Stuart took off his knee-length jogging bottoms and briefs, ready to hit the shower. His cock was already beginning to twitch into life, rising upward in almost imperceptible increments. In all this process, Birgit made no effort to leave the room, causing Allison to wonder exactly what the 'little chat' she'd had with Stuart had involved. Didn't the woman have other duties to perform?

This is wrong, she wanted to say. But Stuart's next words stilled any complaint.

'Birgit's been watching us for the last couple of nights. Isn't that right, Birgit?'

'Yes. I find you both very ... interesting.' The woman's voice had a strong but appealing Scandinavian accent. 'You see, I've known enough submissive women to recognise one when I see one, and everything about you, Allison, tells me you are under your husband's control, and willingly so. And that excites me. It excites me very much.'

Birgit's blue-grey eyes glittered as she took a pace towards Allison. She wore a powdery, floral perfume, but beneath that Allison detected a scent that was pure woman, all musk and desire. Her gaze darted to Stuart, looking for reassurance. It didn't take a genius to work out why the steward had been invited into their cabin; Stuart could have easily taken the tray from her and brought it in himself. At first Allison had thought he might want an audience as he put her through her paces; now she knew he'd really been looking for an accomplice.

'I really need a shower,' Stuart announced, making a show of sniffing his armpits. 'Why don't the two of you get better acquainted while I'm in the bathroom?'

With a backward glance that told Allison he expected her to obey, he strode off in the direction of the en suite, whistling as he went.

Birgit regarded Allison for a few moments without speaking, as if making an assessment. At last, she said, 'Your display posture was very good. I have the feeling your husband has trained you well. Tell me what he does to you.'

'He – he controls me,' Allison began, adding, 'madam.' She didn't know quite why she'd chosen that word, only that it seemed the most appropriate form of address for this formal, tightly reined-in woman. Though Allison suspected that, in the right circumstances, the ice-maiden exterior could quite easily thaw.

'And in what ways does he exert this control?' Birgit had moved to stand close to her, her breath huffing hot against the side of Allison's neck and sending a sharp, thrilling tingle through her body.

'He tells me what to wear, what to eat, how to behave in public. He's put me in restraint when we've been out together, knowing no one will realise what he's done. Sometimes – sometimes he decides whether or not I can have an orgasm ...'

Birgit's finger trailed down over Allison's collarbone, along the top curve of her breast, and settled on her nipple. She'd never been explored so intimately by a woman before, and she hadn't expected that when it happened she'd react as strongly as she did, her nipple tightening, peaking hard beneath Birgit's touch.

'And how does it feel to be denied, little one?'

'It frustrates me.' That was a polite way of putting it; sometimes Stuart would reduce her to a pleading, helpless mess as he took her right to the brink before pulling away, over and again. Her orgasm, when it finally came, was all the sweeter for being deferred, even if it never felt like that at the time. 'But I know he's made his decision, and I have to respect that.'

'So, would you respect the decisions I made?' As she spoke, the steward's finger resumed its teasing explorations, moving down until it rested on her mound, just at the point where her lips divided. Another centimetre, and it would slip into the wet cleft.

Allison realised she'd been holding her breath, willing Birgit to touch her where she needed it most, even though she knew that wasn't likely to happen. With a hissing exhalation, she replied, 'Yes, madam.'

'Good. Very good. So what would you do if I decided I wanted you to play with yourself while I watched?'

What could she do but reply, 'I'd have no choice but to do it, madam.'

Birgit almost looked surprised. Had she expected more in the way of resistance from Allison? If so, Stuart hadn't adequately described the full depths of her submission, or how quickly she could reach a point where all she wanted to do was obey, in order to give pleasure to her master. Or, she hastily amended herself, mistress.

'Do you have anything in the way of toys with you?'

A flush coloured Allison's cheeks as she thought of the accessories Stuart had requested she pack for the voyage. 'Yes, madam.'

'Well, fetch whatever you have. If there's more than one, I'll need to decide what you're going to use on yourself.'

With the bathroom door ajar, Allison could hear the sounds of running water and off-key singing as her husband took a leisurely shower. Did he have any clue as to what was happening? That his wife was hunting in her bedside drawer for her selection of vibrators? Or was he contentedly stroking his cock at the thought of Birgit dominating her, keeping himself on a steady boil in anticipation of his own return to the action?

Allison snatched up her toys, trying not to blush at the breadth of the selection, and took them back to Birgit, who studied each one in turn. She dismissed the waterproof purple toy with the upward curve at the end, designed to stimulate the G-spot, and the flesh-coloured vibe with the realistic veins running down its length and the fat, domed head. Smiling, she selected the slim metal butt-plug and a black bullet vibrator that was one of Stuart's favourite toys to use on Allison, as it never failed to bring her to a swift, squealing orgasm.

'You have lube?' When Allison nodded, Birgit snapped, 'Well, bring it, slut, unless you want this thing going up you without it.'

The way she brandished the butt-plug made Allison's stomach clench with nervous anticipation. She scurried back to the drawer, found what she needed and handed it to her tormentor. Birgit slathered the toy generously, then ordered Allison to get on the bed and raise her knees to her chest.

In that position, she felt exposed and slightly humiliated, as though she was waiting to have her bottom powdered and a nappy fastened in place, but it gave Birgit easy access to the spot she needed. Allison felt a finger, slick with lube, slide over the entrance to her arse, a teasing portent of what was to come.

'Relax, little one,' Birgit ordered, pushing the finger into the tight recesses of Allison's arse. When she'd seen the steward's hand earlier, and noticed how short she kept her nails filed, she'd assumed it was a practical necessity, to prevent them breaking in the course of her duties. Now, she couldn't help wondering if Birgit's severe manicure was carried out for other reasons entirely; the way her finger pushed deeper, exploring Allison's rear passage, suggested she wasn't entirely unfamiliar with this portion of a woman's anatomy.

Abruptly, the finger was withdrawn, and now the cool tip of the butt-plug took its place, pushing through the tight ring of muscle till it was lodged in place. Humiliating as this procedure was, Allison knew it would have been even worse if she'd been asked to insert the plug herself.

As it was, she was going to have to stimulate herself with the vibrator for Birgit's viewing pleasure ...

... and Stuart's, she realised, as her husband strolled back into the cabin bedroom, a white towel knotted around his waist, his dark hair damp and tousled from vigorous towelling. His eyes widened at the sight Allison presented to him, lying on the bed, legs raised, the flange of the butt-plug an obvious target for his gaze where it protruded from her arsehole.

'Wow, Birgit, good going,' he said, sounding impressed. 'What are you going to make her do now?'

Birgit held up the bullet vibe and grinned. 'She takes herself right to the edge with this. If she comes without permission, then it's the worse for her.' She pressed the vibrator into Allison's hand. 'You know what to do, so do it.'

Why don't I just say no? Allison wondered, as she so often did when Stuart suggested some act that butted right up against the limits they'd defined. The truth was she didn't want to. Perverse as it might seem, her pussy only grew wetter at the thought of having to run the toy over her clit for an interested audience. Indeed, as she switched on the vibe, and turned it to the lowest possible setting so as not to bring herself near her peak too soon, part of her wished there was a bigger crowd to witness her in action. Remembering what Stuart had said about handing her over to the ship's captain to play with, she pictured herself sprawled naked on his table at dinner, legs splayed wide to reveal the plug in her arse, as she made herself come in front of all his invited guests. So many people watching, urging her on, telling her all the crude, delicious things they wanted to do to her, the positions they wanted to fuck her in ...

Glancing over to Stuart, she saw his erection was tenting out the towel, and made a mental note to share the fantasy with him when he and Birgit had finished with her. If she still had the wits to bring it to mind, that was; the moment the buzzing vibrator made contact with her clean-shaved sex lips, she knew she was lost. Her master and temporary mistress had demanded that she hold back, refuse to surrender to her orgasm, or suffer the consequences. But that was impossible, and both of them must know it. Need swirled in her belly, stoked by the relentless, humming toy. Her nipples were twin chips of diamond, and when she tweaked one of the tight buds, she felt an answering sensation in her rear hole, clenching hard around the plug that filled her there.

When she touched the head of the vibrator to her clit, it took all her self-control not to come. It would be so easy to just let go, let the hot waves of pleasure sweep her away. But she'd had her orders – no orgasm until Birgit said so – and she was determined to hold out for as long as she could.

'You look fucking amazing,' Stuart, bent close,

whispered into her ear. 'What a good, obedient little slut you are, Allison. I love you so much –' He broke off, registering the soft, steady hum of the vibrator.

'Turn it up, all the way,' he ordered, obviously realising what she'd done. After all, he knew just how powerful the toy could be; he'd used it on her on enough occasions. 'I want to hear that thing on the highest setting.'

As she obeyed, he took one of her nipples between finger and thumb and pinched it till the sensation hovered somewhere between pleasure and pain. Though his smile seemed innocent enough, he knew exactly what she was doing. Try as she might, the extra stimulation, twin assaults on her nipple and clit, were impossible to fight against. Almost sobbing with the shame of being unable to obey her mistress's instruction, Allison came so strongly she thought she might pass out.

Her vision swam, and when it cleared she saw both Stuart and Birgit gazing down at her.

'Oh, little one, didn't I say you weren't allowed to come until I gave my permission?' Birgit's smile was cruel, but her eyes shone with desire. Her fingers flew to the buttons of her uniform blouse, and she began to undo them, one by one. Fixated on the sight of Birgit's breasts, surprisingly large on her slender frame, cradled in a nude-coloured seamless bra designed for function rather than style, Allison didn't at first register her husband reaching for the leather wrist cuffs.

He guided her into a sitting position, then took her wrists and cuffed them together behind her back. The butt-plug was removed from her arse without ceremony.

'It's time for you to pleasure your mistress,' he said, as Birgit continued to undress. The rest of her uniform discarded, Birgit peeled down her knickers and reclined on the bed, regal and glorious in her near-nakedness.

The woman didn't need to issue any instructions; with her thighs lolling wide apart, her wet pink pussy beckoned Allison like a siren call. Shuffling into position, her movements hampered by being in restraint, Allison made herself as comfortable as she could between Birgit's legs.

The first few sweeps of her tongue were tentative, as she accustomed herself to Birgit's unfamiliar taste, roaming over the contours of her sex lips in search of the sensitive pearl that hid within their folds. This wasn't at all how she had expected her morning to go: being made to bring herself to orgasm with a butt-plug buried in her arse, before licking her new friend's pussy, to the obvious delight of her watching husband and master – and all before breakfast, too. But there were worse ways to start the day, Allison thought, beginning to warm to her task, and taking Birgit's soft moans and mutterings of pleasure as proof she was hitting all the right spots. The delights of Madeira, framed by the cabin window, could wait; she had more than enough to explore here. It seemed as though this cruise was going to be a voyage of discovery in more ways than one.

Christmas in the Caribbean
Jacqueline Seewald

Was she really going to do this? Was she actually going to strip off all of her clothes and parade around naked in front of a bunch of total strangers? Had she lost her mind?

Karen Turner was sitting in her car holding onto her steering wheel with a death grip, her knuckles an unhealthy shade of white.

Where was Ginny? Her friend said they'd meet here at one o'clock. Well, it was past that now. This had all been Ginny's idea. She'd dared Karen to come here today.

'Come on, it'll be fun. We've never been to a nudie beach. If it's a bust, excuse the play on words, we can always take a tour of the lighthouse.'

'What kind of guys will be there?'

Ginny smiled. 'Cute, sexy ones I hope. Gotta admit you really get to totally check them out this way.'

'Except they'll be returning the favour.'

'I dare you to do it, Karen. In fact, I double dare you.'

And so it had gone until she finally caved and agreed to meet Ginny at the nude beach. But here she was and no sign of her friend.

She checked out the men. There were a bunch of nude guys engaged in a volleyball game. Karen had never considered herself a voyeur but she had to admit it was a very interesting sight to watch.

People were just sunbathing or splashing around in the water as if it were any ordinary beach on any ordinary summer day. There were older people and younger ones, all naked as on the day they were born.

Should she or shouldn't she? Karen was torn. With shaking hands, she removed her halter top, shorts, panties and sneakers, left her car keys in the visor and headed down the beach.

The sand was hot, burning her feet. She ran so as not to change her mind. She headed straight for the water. The ocean felt wonderful.

Suddenly a beachball whizzed by her head.

'Sorry,' came an abashed apology, 'I meant to send it into your hands.'

She blinked. Standing not far from her was the handsomest man she'd ever seen. His tan was accentuated by sun-streaked hair and he had the body of Michaelangelo's David, all lean muscle and well-endowed. She let out an appreciative sigh.

'That's all right,' she said, tossing the ball back to him.

'I'm Jim Driscoll,' he said. He had a nice Western twang to his voice.

After a brief pause, she finally remembered her own name and told him.

'First time here?' he asked.

'Does it show?'

'You're pale.'

She found herself blushing. 'I came here on a dare from a friend.'

'Swimming without clothes is liberating,' he said with a big sexy smile.

'I just feel embarrassed.'

'Believe me, you've got nothing to feel embarrassed about.' He looked her up and down meaningfully.

She could feel her face start to burn. 'I've got to go,' she said. 'This was a mistake.' She took off back to her car like a gazelle.

'Wait!' he called after her.

She was breathless from her sprint to the car when he caught up with her.

'I want your phone number,' he said.

She shook her head. 'I don't think that would be a good idea.'

'Sure, it would. Give me your number. I'll phone you. We'll have a proper date anywhere you like. I'll even wear clothes.'

She was hurriedly dressing now. 'I don't know,' she said.

'I'm not a sex fiend, pervert or voyeur. I'm an attorney. Of course, some people might say that was worse. Come over to my car and I'll give you my business card. Will you call me?'

When she didn't answer him, he walked away. She thought that was the end of it. But, driving down the highway, Karen looked in the rearview mirror and caught sight of a car tailing hers. Her eyes narrowed. It was him! There was no question about it. He was actually following her home. Was he a stalker? No, she didn't have that impression of him.

All the way back to her apartment, he stayed with her. She was nervous but also excited. Nothing like this had ever happened to her before.

When she parked her car, he was there beside her.

'I should call the police,' she said to him angrily.

'We didn't finish our conversation,' he said in a calm voice.

'Do you follow every woman you meet?'

'Only you.' His eyes caressed her face.

'I can't believe you actually followed me all this distance just to arrange a date!'

'I'm persistent. It's one of my best qualities. I'm also persuasive. That's what makes me a good lawyer.'

'Well, I'm a nurse, and I think you probably need professional help.'

He gave her that big sexy grin of his. 'I think you're just the one to give it to me.'

'You're impossible.'

'People have said that before. I don't suppose you'd invite me in for a cold drink? It's mighty hot out today and it sure was a long drive. I'm awfully thirsty.'

And so, thinking she really ought to see a psychiatrist herself, she invited a stranger into her apartment – and ended up offering him a whole lot more than a glass of lemonade.

'You have a nice place here,' he said, looking around, as she quickly went into the small kitchen area to the refrigerator.

'Thank you.'

'Nice paintings.'

Few people noticed. She found herself unaccountably pleased.

'Who's the artist?'

'Those are mine,' she said. 'I dabble a little. Helps me relax. My work at the hospital sometimes leaves me tense.'

'You're very talented,' he said, studying the landscape she'd hung over the couch in the living room.

'You like art?' she asked, returning with the lemonade glasses.

'I do. Of course, I don't know all that much about it.'

'I'm glad you like my work,' she said, thinking she sounded stiff and awkward.

'I know what I like, and I especially like the artist.'

She watched him swallow his drink, his throat strong and masculine. He oozed testosterone. She tried not to stare at him but found him fascinating. Their eyes met and held. He had riveting blue eyes. She hadn't noticed that before.

'So what kind of law do you practise?' She hoped she didn't sound as nervous as she felt.

'Civil stuff, dull corporate work.'

'No criminal cases?'

'Nothing so exciting.' He took another swallow of his lemonade. 'Good stuff,' he said.

'I squeezed the lemons myself.'

'I'm impressed.' Could blue eyes be so warm? She never would have guessed it.

'I'm into health and fitness.'

He gave her an appraising look. 'I'm not surprised.'

His smile was dazzling, potent, as steady and sure as a sunrise. He was too attractive, his smile too seductive.

'You should go,' she said.

'And end this uplifting conversation?' He put down his drink on the coffee table.

Then he took her hand in his. The touch of his finger-tips against her skin made her feel both hot and cold at once. She trembled from this merest of intimacies. It was as if a volcano were erupting in her blood. She was frightened, not by him, but by her reaction to him. She regarded herself as cool where men were concerned, but at this moment her emotions, her nerve endings, were raw and exposed. She had somehow allowed herself to feel attracted to a complete stranger, one who seemed to comprehend exactly how she felt, judging by his expression. This had never happened to her before and it was frightening.

She felt his warm breath on her cheek and was jolted by an electric reaction that sent heat rushing to her face. She made herself pull away from him, although it wasn't easy.

'There is something you could do for me before I leave.'

'And what would that be?'

His eyes sparkled mischievously. 'I'm afraid, if I told you, you might hit me.'

'I don't go to bed with men I barely know, if that's what you're thinking.'

'Too bad,' he said with that special smile.

Suddenly his body moved fluidly against her own. She was in his arms before she knew it, and he was kissing her, his mouth warm and moist against hers, his arms wrapped tightly around her.

'I don't believe this is a good idea.' Her voice sounded husky and breathless to her own ears.

'It's the best idea I've ever had.'

He captured her lips, his mouth hard yet soft at the same time. And she felt as if she were melting like butter. He tasted of tart lemon and some indefinable male essence, provocative and madly disturbing. She fought the pleasure, struggling against the passionate need beginning to build inside her. The blood surged through her veins, throbbing in her ears. She heard the pounding of his heart as he pressed her against him. Her own heart galloped in response. He slid his hands down her body to cup her derrière. His mouth met hers with passion, kissing her deeper, harder.

'That was some kiss,' she said breathlessly, as she broke away.

'You're not so bad yourself.' He drew her into his arms again.

Never before had she trembled with such yearning. Never had she felt so languid or dizzy with the force of desire. She was a strong woman. Why was she suddenly feeling so weak? She placed the palm of her hand against his hard chest, attempting to put some distance between them, breaking the contact. But his hand came up to hold the back of her head firmly. Then his tongue snaked out and seductively outlined her lips with its tip. She found herself gasping for breath.

Ever so slowly his tongue insinuated itself into her mouth, touching hers, rubbing hers, mating in an erotic rhythm. She couldn't think. She saw the sensuous curve of his mouth and her eyes drifted shut. Nothing existed but this moment, this drugging kiss, wild, wonderful beyond belief. She was light-headed, burning in an inferno of ultimate ecstasy and desire, responding to him as she had never responded to any man before. His hard chest, pressed against the softness of her breasts, made them feel full and exquisitely sensitive. Her nipples tightened, straining against the fabric of his knit shirt.

She felt the power of his hard, thick erection as it pressed boldly against her core. It thrilled her, but it also sobered her. Fear set in; survival instincts took over. What madness was this? What was she allowing to happen here? This man was an unknown quantity.

She sensed he would be a wonderful lover but that could not be. She pushed him away, pulling herself free of his embrace.

'I don't know you,' she said. 'And you don't know me.'

'But I want to know you, and not just in the biblical sense. I trust my gut instincts. You and I are meant to be together.'

'You really think so?' she asked. She was afraid this man was just a stranger looking for a quick sex fix. 'How do I know I can trust you?'

'How do you know you can trust anyone?'

'You really are persuasive.'

He smiled again, that heart-stopping smile of his. 'I told you. See how truthful I am?'

She found him overwhelmingly desirable. Had the kisses they'd shared moved him the way it did her?

The passion he'd stirred made mush of her brain. But what had he felt? Probably nothing more than momentary lust.

As if in answer to her question, he pulled her into his arms again. This time there was nothing gentle about the kiss. Her thoughts muddled as pure, raw attraction sizzled between them. He ran his hand over her breasts and her nipples stood at attention. His mouth fastened on one engorged nipple, sucking through the thin material of her halter top and sending shivers down her spine. Then he moved himself against her, between her legs, his arousal hard and determined. She pressed a trembling hand against his erection and he let out a hoarse groan. He wanted her all right, but she wanted him too. There was no denying the quivering low in her belly.

His hands ran slowly over her bottom. Between her legs, her swollen flesh wept with need. He slipped off her shorts and panties.

'God, you're hot,' he whispered into her ear as his hands caressed her intimately.

Somehow, they made it to her bedroom, touching each other everywhere. It wasn't long before they were both naked, sweaty and breathless.

There wasn't much in the way of foreplay. They were both too hungry, too volatile, too wild with desire. As if in a dream, she groped into her nightstand, then ripped the small foil packet she found there. She rolled it over the sensitive flesh that was the core of his male power. His arousal was like a pulsating velvet fist.

He moaned as if in pain. And then he was inside of her, part of her, joining her in an exquisite torment of pleasure and sensation as he moved in and out sinuously. Finally he began to thrust deep and hard. She matched his rhythm as they took each other higher and higher still. And finally they came simultaneously, and she shattered, panting and breathless. It was incredible! She cried out in exquisite pleasure. She'd never experienced such a powerful orgasm.

It was only later, when she was dressing again, that the doubts and fears returned. What had she done? Was she insane? She'd had sex with a total stranger!

He watched her intently. 'You've got one sensational body.'

'So do you,' she said, not meeting his eyes.

'I know what you're thinking, but you're wrong. You and I didn't just have sex, we made love. We belong together.'

* * *

Karen Turner was driving home from work when The Dixie Chicks sashayed over the airwaves singing 'Cowboy Take Me Away'.

She sighed. 'Don't I wish.'

She was still thinking about the song when she arrived at the condo that was now home to her and Jim. They had been very happy here since they moved in together. Jim was right, they'd been destined to develop a meaningful relationship.

If anyone had told her that a lifelong New Jersey resident would meet a Montana cowboy and fall passionately in love, she would have laughed. Yet here she was, completely committed to him. She hoped Jim felt the same way. He wasn't the kind of man who expressed his emotions easily. But it was obvious he cared about her. She just wished he would say the words, tell her how much he loved her.

She kicked off her shoes and leaned back on the couch. She had switched on the radio to relax with some more country music, her favourite since falling in love with Jim. If only he could take her away like the song said. They both worked so hard, caught up in their careers. They never seemed to have enough time or money to take a real vacation. That would be her idea of heaven. On a raw autumn day like this, she especially dreamed of visiting someplace exotic and romantic, a paradise.

Jim arrived home as she was putting dinner together. He gave her a warm kiss that she felt right down to her toes.

'How were things at the hospital today?'

'Hectic in OR.'

'So who works harder, you nurses or the doctors?'

'We do, naturally.'

Jim smiled, betraying a dimple in his right cheek.

'Oh, you don't believe me? Careful or I'll start telling lawyer jokes.'

'Now you're playing dirty, Red,' he said, his blue eyes twinkling bright and clear as the Montana sky.

'We redheads are temperamental,' she said. 'Just keep that in mind.' As she poked his chest with her forefinger, he caught her hand and began kissing each fingertip. 'Now who's playing dirty?'

'Me,' he agreed with an easy smile. 'And darlin', don't you forget it.'

'You men like to take charge, don't you, cowboy?'

Jim yanked off his navy-striped tie. Then he pulled Karen into his arms and gave her a bone-melting kiss.

'If you think you can turn me on at this time of the day, forget it. I'm dead tired,' she said in a husky, breathless voice.

'I'm tired too, but not dead.'

'Where do you get the energy?'

He ran his hand through the thick sandy brown hair that fell in waves over his forehead. 'Can't help it. Whenever I see you I start thinking sexy thoughts. You turn me on.'

She pushed him away. 'Dinner's going to burn if I don't stay in the kitchen.'

He let out a deep sigh. 'Can't you shut off the oven and come to bed with me for a while?'

'Aren't you hungry?'

'Yeah, I'm starving, but not for food.' He pulled her against him and let her feel the lean, hard lines of his well-muscled body. And, for a while, she forgot everything but the pleasure they shared together.

Pure raw attraction sizzled between them. He slipped his hand around the back of her neck and angled her head so that his mouth came to hers. Touched. Brushed. And lingered. His kiss muddled her brain.

She unbuttoned his shirt and slid her hand down his bare chest, feeling the rapid beat of his heart. Memory flooded back of how they were together. The slow eating hunger that was always there had a new urgency. They pulled at each other's clothes. He lowered his head and sampled her breast, sucking and licking her nipples. She ran her hand over the front of his trousers. Then she unzipped them and pulled them off, and slid her hand into his boxer shorts. He stripped off her panties, then managed a hoarse groan as she wrapped her fingers around his penis.

'God, I want you,' he said.

Suddenly, he was pushing her to the floor, taking her in a wild, elemental way. There was friction. Pressure. Thrust after penetrating thrust.

She matched his rhythm. When they could go no

higher, and neither could take any more, he brought them both to a powerful, pulsating climax. They lay entwined, breathless and slick with sweat.

* * *

Later that evening, Karen browsed the internet looking for interesting travel websites. They could both take time off for a vacation this Christmas, if only she were able to find some terrific but inexpensive holiday destination. She was still paying off student loans, and there were the payments on her car. She had two younger siblings, so she hadn't wanted to ask her parents for anything. As for Jim, his mother was a widow. She and Jim's younger brother ran the family ranch, but it was proving to be a financial drain. Jim sent them all the money he could spare. And he still drove the same old Chevy pick-up he'd come East in.

He worked long hours, often six days a week, at a demanding law firm. He was ambitious and hard-working, which Karen admired, but they rarely had time together to just relax and enjoy each other. Mostly there was too little sleep and too much stress for both of them. What they needed was more hot sex and less work.

Surfing the web was discouraging. Everything that sounded good was expensive. Then, just as she was about to give up, a site popped up that took her interest: CONTEST: WINNER GETS A FREE CRUISE FOR ADVERTISING OUR COMPANY. The more she read, the more excited she became.

* * *

'A Caribbean cruise in the middle of winter,' Ginny sighed. 'If we hadn't been best friends since fourth grade, Karen, I'd be jealous. Come to think of it, I'm jealous anyway. Spending Christmas in the Caribbean, what could be better?'

Karen turned to her best friend and smiled. 'I know you're really happy for us. Besides, green is definitely not your best colour and so hard to properly accessorise.'

'We're both glad you're getting away.' Rick Varner placed one arm around Ginny. 'To our best friends, Karen and Jim,' Rick toasted, lifting a glass of beer in tribute.

'Thanks for driving us to the airport,' Jim said. But he was slow to raise his glass, something Karen did not miss.

'We had to wish you bon voyage,' Ginny said. 'I still can't believe you won that contest.'

'Neither can I,' Karen said. 'When Mr Brenner called and said mine was the winning entry, I was beyond thrilled. I've never won anything before.'

'I do wish we could go with you,' Ginny said.

'Me too,' Karen agreed.

They all got along so well together. Karen and Jim had

introduced Ginny to Rick, who was an attorney at Jim's office. Karen was really happy that things had worked out well between their friends.

As for herself, she had felt the chemistry between her and Jim from the beginning. She'd never found another man as attractive. Jim was strong yet gentle, handsome outside as well as inside where it counted most.

Karen was cheerful during the plane ride to Miami, but Jim was uncharacteristically silent. Finally, she asked him if something was bothering him.

'Guess I'm just a tad cynical about getting something for nothing,' he said. 'I've learned in life there is no free lunch.'

She found herself annoyed as well as disappointed in his attitude. Was he being a male chauvinist, critical because she had taken the initiative? 'People win contests all the time. Please tell me you're going to keep an open mind and enjoy yourself.'

'Let's just see how it goes,' Jim said with a frown.

A short, thin man met them at the airport in Miami and introduced himself as Gregory Brenner. He was a well-dressed, middle-aged gentleman who shook their hands with a damp, limp grip reminiscent of a dead catfish. He handed Karen a large silver carrying bag with the name RAYBELL'S stencilled on it in big black letters. 'You'll be expected to carry this with you wherever you stop off. At each port, display this tote bag.'

'And the reason for that would be?' Jim asked, his eyes narrowing.

Brenner pulled at his collar and cleared his throat. 'She'll be advertising Raybell's and the fact that she's the winner of our contest. It's good publicity. Not much for us to ask considering you're getting a free vacation worth thousands of dollars.'

Karen gave Jim a hard look. 'Of course I'm perfectly happy to comply.'

As they were driven to the dock, Jim looked grim. 'Can't trust a man who doesn't look you straight in the eye,' he said.

Why was he behaving so critically? She decided to just ignore his attitude.

Karen was thrilled when she saw the cruise ship for the first time. It was so large and beautiful! She soon discovered there were flowers in their room courtesy of Mr Brenner. True, it wasn't a stateroom but it was quite comfortable, neat and clean. She was soon standing on deck beside Jim and watching the crewmen cast off. The tropical breeze lifted her hair as the blood-red sun set on the horizon.

They enjoyed their time at sea, soaking up the sun at poolside and sipping planter's punch while listening to the steel-drum band play island music. The meals were excellent, including lavish midnight buffets after music and dancing. They even held hands and kissed like teenagers while they watched a romantic comedy in the movie theatre. There were also other couples to talk with, whose company they came to enjoy. The vacation was everything she had hoped for. Certainly Jim had nothing to complain about.

Their itinerary promised exotic locations. They were to sail the Western Caribbean. Karen was thrilled when they disembarked at their first port of call, Cozumel in Mexico. They decided to take a cab into town and from there go snorkelling. They relaxed on the small boat where rum drinks and beer were served. The diving gear was provided for them and a crewman competently led their group off a reef. Beneath the ocean were spectacular drop-offs, walls and swim-throughs, beautiful coral gardens where she and Jim observed large pelagic fish and dolphins. It seemed as if the fish were lit up by neon lights, their colours brilliant and iridescent. She felt like a honeymooner.

After they returned downtown, they had lunch at a small restaurant decorated with Mayan artifacts. The area was packed with colourful shops, markets and tourists. Then they walked to a lagoon reserve full of turtles, surrounded by a botanical garden. Jim kissed and hugged her as they admired the hibiscus and other tropical flowers. Karen felt like a princess in a fairy tale.

Later they caught a tour bus. The Punta Celarin Lighthouse had a mystical quality. There was extraordinary music produced by wind whistling through the encrusted shells of the walls. It made her shiver with an odd sensual longing.

San Gervasio, an archaeological site, was the only excavated ruin on the island. There they found a temple built in honour of Ixchel, the Mayan god of fertility.

'Being here will bring you children,' their guide assured them. 'It is good luck.'

'A child wouldn't be so bad,' Jim responded, a sparkle in his eye. He rubbed his hand provocatively along the side of her breast.

No, having a baby wouldn't be bad at all. They hadn't even talked about marriage or considered starting a family, but maybe it was time they did. Maybe she worried too much about money. If they did get married and have a baby, they would manage.

With Jim's arm around her, they left the tour bus and walked through town back towards the harbour.

'Sun's setting. Brilliant flame just like your hair. Maybe I should get us a cab,' he said. 'You must be tired after all we've done today. In fact, I think we could both use a little time in the sack.' He wiggled his eyebrows suggestively, making her laugh.

He turned to look back, then suddenly stiffened, his face becoming all hard lines and planes.

'What's the matter?'

'That guy back there. He was behind us when we

went to the restaurant and again when we caught the tour bus. He's following us.'

'Are you sure?' She turned to take a quick look.

'I recognise him. He doesn't look like a local or a tourist. See how he's dressed in that white suit?'

'Why would he want to follow us?'

Jim didn't comment but quickly flagged down the first taxi that passed.

Karen had all but forgotten the incident by the time they were taken ashore at Grand Cayman Island. They decided to go snorkelling again. The water was warm, with very little current. They began snorkelling at the edge of a coral reef in ten to twenty feet of water and saw many reef fish, coral heads and a huge green moray eel.

Their next stop was Sting Ray City. Here the water was only three or four feet deep and the rays numerous. They were provided with squid to feed the rays and carefully instructed how to go about it. Karen thought the rays were like big cats rubbing up against her and nuzzling her back and legs. The next thing she knew, her cowboy was imitating the rays. She felt a rush of desire.

'I wish we could just get it on right here and now,' she whispered.

'Me too,' he said, 'but we might just shock a lot of folks on the beach.' Still, he rubbed his hand back and forth slowly and sensually between her legs below the water level until she came under his touch.

She moaned and he kissed her nose.

They had a fish lunch at the harbour front. Karen admired the gingerbread-style buildings lining the area. She was just reaching into her bag for her camera when someone shoved into her. The carrying bag was wrenched from her shoulder. She let out a cry of dismay.

'Are you all right?' Jim questioned.

'Fine, but that man stole my bag!'

'Not for long.' Jim took off after him.

'No, forget the bag! I don't need it.' She was truly frightened for Jim. The bag suddenly seemed unimportant.

Jim ignored her and kept going, right down a narrow alley. She had trouble keeping up with his long-legged strides; she was panting and breathless. She saw Jim had got her carry-all back. But the thief was reaching into his pants pocket for something. Karen screamed a warning. Jim brought his fist crashing into the man's jaw, knocking him to the ground. Then he took her arm and they fled back to the street.

'We ought to find the local police,' she said as they ran.

'No time. We'll miss the last tender back to the ship if we do. I'll talk to the captain.'

Jim was late getting back to the cabin, and his eyes were shadows.

'What did the captain say?'

'He had me talk with the head security officer. Darlin', it might be a good idea if you don't carry that bag at the next port.'

'But I promised Mr Brenner I would.'

'Do what you want.' Jim's jaw jutted out and his eyes were like shards of ice on a winter lake.

He hardly spoke to her that evening. When they finally returned to their cabin, Karen felt as turbulent as a storm at sea.

'Are you actually blaming me for what happened?' she said.

'I just wish you hadn't accepted this free vacation.'

'You are holding me responsible. How unfair!'

He didn't respond, but left the cabin for a long walk. She hated it when he refused to discuss their differences. Suddenly, the pleasure and magic she'd felt about winning the trip were completely gone.

Jim met with the security officer again the next day, taking her bag with him. When he returned, he refused to talk about what they had discussed. He simply returned the bag and told her that she could take it with her if she wanted. She noted that the lining had been partly cut open. That night, for the first time since they began living together, they slept on opposite sides of the bed with their backs turned to each other. She was awake most of the night, choking back tears of silent rage. She'd never felt so alone or unhappy. She wanted him to make love to her, but she wasn't going to make the first move.

At Ocho Rios, Jamaica, they stayed with a tour group for a trip to Fern Gully and the Botanical Gardens, with the final stop at Dunn's River Falls. The vans were clean and air-conditioned and the guide well versed. But Karen was too depressed and tired to enjoy the beautiful scenery.

They explored the waterfall, which flowed like buttermilk. The falls were very steep and treacherous to climb. However, once they began, there was no turning back. The water was fast, pounding, and it was difficult to tell just where she was putting her foot down. Karen cried out as she lost her balance, certain that she was going to fall to her death. Jim caught her and held her tightly in his arms. She began to cry, the dam bursting on all the tears she'd held back the night before. Jim kissed her tears away. She buried her face against his chest.

'Karen, I love you. I'm sorry I acted the way I did. I didn't mean to hurt you. I just got so angry. I kept thinking you put yourself in danger needlessly.' He caressed her cheek and kissed her hand.

'I promise not to let anything or anyone come between us ever again,' she said. 'I love you too. Our love is worth more than anything else in the world.'

'I've been acting like a dang fool,' he said.

Karen felt she ought to feel embarrassed by the spectacle she'd made of herself but somehow it didn't seem important. What mattered was that she and Jim had reopened the lines of communication between them, and Jim had finally told her that he loved her.

Just as they began walking along the congested street

towards the harbour, someone pushed into her, snatched her Raybell bag and took off. Karen had a sense of déjà vu. But this time, at Jim's urging, the bag had been left empty. Two men who looked very much like police ran after the thief.

Karen turned to Jim. 'I suppose you're going to tell me what that was about?'

He gave her an infuriatingly smug smile. 'Ask me real nice tonight in bed, and I just might explain.'

And that was exactly what she did. After spraying her favourite perfume on her throat and wrists, she slipped into bed in a black silk nightgown. Jim removed his well-washed denim jeans that fit him like a second skin and wasted no time joining her.

'You look beautiful,' he said. 'Your eyes are moonbeams.'

'Forget about buttering me up right now. You were going to tell me why people kept trying to steal my bag?'

He kissed her neck and she breathed in the clean male scent of him. 'Well, it seems you had some diamonds sewn into the lining of that bag.'

'What?'

'Yep, they were worth a few dollars. That fella Brenner and his company are part of a laundering operation. Drugs sent north and sold, money converted to gems and smuggled back to the drug dealers. You were being used as a mule.'

She groaned. 'So I didn't really win a free vacation?'

'Afraid not, darlin'. But we did help the authorities catch some lowdown thievin' varmints. Promise me that in the future, when you want a vacation, we'll budget for it. Sometimes when a thing is too good to be true, that's exactly what it is.'

'So what can I get for free?'

He gave her his most appealing smile. 'I'm right glad you asked that question, ma'am,' he drawled. 'I aim to show you.'

She stared into his eyes. He lowered his head so that his mouth touched hers, brushed back and forth over soft, warm flesh. She made a tiny incoherent sound and her hand moved to his shoulders, anchoring him to her. She brought her mouth back to his, pressing, deepening the contact, drinking in the wonderful taste of him in huge gulps. When he finally raised his head, they were both trembling and breathless.

'That was wonderful,' she gasped.

'Glad you thought so too. Karen, honey, I think it's time we made it legal. I want to marry you.'

'Oh, yes, yes, yes!' She threw her arms around him and kissed him enthusiastically with all the desire and passion in her heart.

He kissed her again, before moving between her legs. She spread her thighs as his clever mouth found her, and drifted away on a cloud of pure pleasure.

She felt his rock-hard erection pressing against her, pressing into her.

'You're hot and moist and ready,' he said.

'For you, always.'

He bared her breasts and began licking and sucking her nipples. She went wild, cupping him, then rubbing his aroused flesh. She'd never wanted him more, never desired him more. No, nothing was ever going to come between them again.